RJ Scott & Meredith Russell

Capture the Sun

Sapphire Cay book 5
RJ Scott and Meredith Russell
Copyright © 2015 RJ Scott and Meredith Russell
Copyright © 2015 Love Lane Books

First eBook publication: 2014

Cover design by Meredith Russell
Edited by RJ Locksley and Erika Orrick

All Rights Reserved:

RJ Scott & Meredith Russell

Dedication

For our family and friends.

And a special thank you to Erika who makes magic. *We love you.*

Contents

RJ Scott & Meredith Russell

Chapter 1

Mitch Stone sipped at very weak whiskey and water and people-watched. He'd done the rounds twice already, flirted with the women, talked sports with the men, and every other cliché under the sun. Now he was hiding to give himself some time to think and staying as sober as he could while having a drink permanently in his hand.

It's Christmas Eve, live a little.

"Why are you hiding over here?" his senior manager asked with a frown. She was looking a little glassy-eyed, and the champagne glass in her hand was nearly empty.

Mitch lifted his glass in a toast and smiled easily. He liked Doris, with all her power suits and her impossibly high heels. Tonight she appeared relaxed, and it was a good look on her. "I'm just taking a breather." He wasn't going to lie to her. She was uncannily quick to see through anyone's bullshit.

"Don't stay here," she admonished. She grabbed a new champagne flute from one of the waiters and sipped at it. "I'm going out to find some fun. I'll find you some while I'm at it."

"Don't—" She'd gone before he could say what he wanted to say. Mitch watched her weave expertly through the groups forming around the small tables and toward a particularly gorgeous young man who had caught Mitch's eye more than once tonight.

He must be a party favor, young guys and girls brought in to add glitter and romance, slim young girls with short dresses and scarlet lipstick who pandered to any man at a loose end in the crowd, escorts who were available if you needed them. That was how it worked at big seasonal parties like this one. Since there were women who might need that little something, this particular party also included a whole team of cute men who sashayed and mingled, with alcohol they didn't drink and promise in their expressions. They were all included in with the party, no cost involved.

This young guy, all bright-eyed with soft spiky hair, was so slim it almost seemed unnatural, but he had a good ass, a nice handful, and he was just as happy casting glances back at Mitch. Doris chatted to him, placing a hand on the young guy's shoulder and leaning in to say something into his ear. He laughed at whatever Doris was saying and looked over at Mitch.

Oh shit, no. Is Doris setting me up with one of the party favors? Like hell that's happening.

The young man, who must be in his early twenties, nodded his head and spoke to Doris, all the while looking at Mitch, and Mitch ducked away before the man decided he needed an escort tonight. He was here on business, and the last thing he needed was sex.

This was Mitch Stone's night. He was at the Haddison-Walker Christmas Eve party, and he was selling his brand to anyone who wanted him. Wearing charcoal Armani, with his loafers polished to a high sheen, his favorite Armani shirt, and a rich blue tie, he *knew* he looked good. He looked completely the part of the guy who deserved to be here.

"Hey, Mitch," a CEO with his wife clinging to his arm called out.

Mitch nodded as he walked past like he had somewhere to be, when in fact all he wanted was another quiet corner to people-watch. He'd schmoozed with that particular CEO—he already had the man's card in his pocket. He might be new to the company, but brokering the Haddison-

Walker deal with Davis was the kind of news that left people slapping his back and asking how the hell he had done it. Everyone who had ever guided the two companies in any kind of joint project knew just how hard it was to get a positive outcome. The CEOs were brothers yet hated each other. Their passions were quick to ignite to temper, but somehow Mitch Stone had managed the near impossible. He'd worked out a joint marketing deal that was beneficial to both sides.

I am a confident, capable marketing executive, he'd told himself before he came down to the party from his room. He had to believe that, otherwise he would fail to capitalize on the big win and be just another low-level marketing assistant sliding into obscurity.

Mitch wanted to be *the* marketing fixer, using every skill he'd learned from ten years with Dylan Gray Senior about contracts and terms. He needed to be the first one Miami companies thought of when they wanted help. And he had to be the one who matched person to product or group to sponsor. His unique firefighting style of marketing expertise, from graffiti to flash mobs, was making waves in the business world here in Miami. He had his finger on the pulse and Dolphins tickets in his pocket along with cards and notes from prospective clients.

There was good money here tonight, people in all kinds of business wanting his particular skills. Companies wanted the edge; they wanted young and new and fresh. This party was *that* kind of party — networking, smiling, hugging, and air kisses with good food and excellent wine.

"Mitch Stone! Didn't think I would see you here." A voice from his left had him turning. "Thought you'd be too busy out spending your bonus."

Mitch shook hands with someone he recognized, but for the life of him he couldn't place the name of the man. He was probably one of the team who had been up in New York on long-term assignment and he wouldn't be the first face Mitch couldn't put a name to.

"Thought I'd take Haddison-Walker up on their invite," Mitch said. He wasn't going to share the real reason he was here. Just that he needed to mingle and get himself out there to avoid the thought of doing fuck-all over Christmas.

The guy took a step back and thrust a very pretty woman forward. She had a big baby-bump and looked serene in the *pregnant-lady* version of a little black dress.

"This is Melinda, my wife," the guy said proudly.

Mitch air-kissed and said all the right things. "When are you due?"

"End of March," Melinda said. "Jerry is so excited. He's like a kid at Christmas."

Jerry! That's right, Jerry something-or-other.

Jerry pulled his wife in close and squeezed her. "Why wouldn't I be? I'm here at the party of the year with the gorgeous woman who's carrying our baby and whom I couldn't love more. What could possibly beat this?" He was beaming and maybe just a little drunk. Hell, he was clearly so besotted with his life at the moment that Mitch felt a twinge of irrational jealousy. *I'm happy with the deal and the bonus and the kudos, that's enough…*

Not that he wanted a woman by his side or, perish the thought, a baby on its way. But to have someone on Christmas Eve must be kind of nice. Maybe one of these sexy but drunken marketing execs making more noise than they needed to was gay and fancied a hookup that would smooth Mitch into Christmas Day.

"We have to go," Melinda apologized. She placed a hand on her swollen belly. "We called a cab. I get so tired."

"Nice to meet you. Good luck with the baby," Mitch said with an accompanying smile. He even managed to push genuine emotion into his voice, despite the alcohol in his system and the headache that threatened at his temples.

Jerry took Melinda and the two vanished into the throng, leaving Mitch at loose ends. Fixers like him didn't stand around waiting for people to come to them; they went into the crowd like sharks.

Do I really have to? On Christmas Eve? Haven't I got enough business for a while?

Jerry appeared back at his side, a bright purple wrap over his arm. "I meant to tell you… I have a client in need of a photo shoot, large budget. I'm worried I'm going to drop the ball on this one, what with Melinda and everything. I'm trying to pull in Bruno Cash, but he needs some persuading." He handed over a bright pink Post-It note with some scribbled details. "They're looking for standard stuff, so maybe it isn't your kind of thing, and I realize you're busy with the Haddison-Walker/Davis thing. But the company is looking for something a bit special in the way of a survivalist tents, fires, island-type thing. I'll finish all the groundwork, but I was hoping you'd be my backup if Melinda is early."

Mitch nodded. How likely was it that Melinda would be early? Anyway, he could do with making a few friends at the company.

"Happy to help if I can," Mitch said automatically. Actually, it sounded like nothing he would be interested in working on, but he wouldn't pass on it just yet, not when he wasn't sober. *Never make a drunken decision*, his mom admonished him in his thoughts, and he remembered he hadn't called her yet to wish her Merry Christmas.

Mitch made a show of pocketing the Post-It. As soon as Jerry left, Mitch pushed the request to the back of his mind and turned determinedly toward the groups of men and woman who needed his special skills. He schmoozed with the best of them, and only when he'd done enough talking did he wander out to the balcony with the ocean view and turn his thoughts to the Post-It note and what Jerry had said.

The sea, beaches, camps, fires — all the thoughts in his head swirled around to one person, as they always did. His ex-lover, Dylan, of the come-to-bed blue eyes. *He has an island.* And if Mitch fixed something between Dylan and this client, then that meant he had a valid reason to see Dylan again and maybe check out just what this boyfriend of Dylan's was like, Liam or Luke or something beginning with an L. He resolved to pass on details of the island to Jerry anyway, and maybe he would make himself available as a replacement if needed. Any excuse to visit Sapphire Cay. And Dylan.

"Hot in there, isn't it?"

Mitch sighed inwardly. He was done with the networking. He just wanted to stay out here in the cool night air with his crystal tumbler of whiskey and imagine Dylan's response if Mitch asked to use his island. *He'll probably charge me double.*

He cast a look sideways and his irritation became even more pronounced when he recognized the slim guy Doris was talking to next to him, all sultry-eyed and wet-lipped.

"No. But thank you," Mitch said firmly. He might not have had actual sex in nearly two months. But, shit, the last thing he needed was the sex on offer from one of the party favors.

The young man — dark brown eyes and beautiful in an angular way — simply blinked up at him. Or across to him. Actually, for a twink he was a good five ten, and on closer inspection he looked a little older than the young guys hired in. Still, he was dressed in tight pants that left nothing to the imagination and a white shirt that strained over a slim, muscled body.

"Sorry?" he said and looked confused.

"Thank you, but no," Mitch repeated. The young man looked behind him, clearly checking to see if

Mitch was looking at someone else. Mitch sighed. "I don't want what you're offering."

"Sorry." The guy frowned. "Doris said I should talk to you. I was just commenting on the heat inside." He held out his hand. "I'm—"

Instinctively Mitch raised his hand and shook his head. He wasn't interested in names. Not ones of escorts, anyway. If the escort finished his introduction, Mitch didn't hear. *I have had more to drink than I thought.*

Instead, as the man spoke, all Mitch could focus on was the sound, deep and sexy. "Okay. So who offered you something you didn't want?" the stranger asked curiously.

Mitch sighed tiredly. "Half the guys like you in the room."

The man shifted so his back was against the rail and sipped what looked like cranberry and ice. "Like me?"

"Here for the party."

"We're all here for the party, or am I wrong?"

"You know what I mean." God, was this guy being deliberately obtuse? A couple other people joined them on the balcony, and Mitch suddenly felt incredibly awkward. What if a potential client saw him talking to one of the escorts? Time to head out. "Nice to meet you," he said without meaning it. Then he stalked back into the crowd and made straight for the exit of the large ballroom.

He went to the nearest elevators and pressed the up button. He wasn't the only one at this party who was staying overnight, but he was probably the only one going back to his room this early with the express purpose of spending Christmas Eve on his own.

Chapter 2

As soon as Mitch was back in room 2512, he flung off his jacket and slumped into the chair at the window with three of the small bottles from the mini bar in his hand. Dylan and his island were front and center in his head, and he blamed Jerry for putting him there. He downed the alcohol and stared into the dark until finally he couldn't see any reason why phoning Dylan this late on Christmas Eve wasn't a brilliant idea. He pulled out his cell and searched for Sapphire Cay, finding the number quickly and looking at the website. The site was pretty, functional, but beyond that, it was kind of difficult to find the number on the tiny screen and there was no Facebook page. Finally, after much squinting at his iPhone, he found a number, and before he could second-guess himself, he connected a call. The island would be the perfect backdrop for what Jerry needed, Mitch was sure of it. He could leave a message—strike while the iron was hot, so to speak.

Evidently the main number wasn't connected to an answering machine this late at night but direct through to a cell phone. Dylan's cell. *Fuck.*

"What's wrong? Is it Dad?" Dylan asked instead of identifying himself. He sounded panicked, and Mitch felt instant guilt.

"Dylan, that you?" He'd drunk enough to be on the cusp of slurring his words, and he focused hard on speaking. "I need to book your island," he added.

Dylan made a sound of annoyance. "What the hell, Mitch?"

"Got a contract with models, lots of 'em, and Jerry said he needed an island. Then I thought, Dylan has a freaking island. And it's Christmas Eve, and I was thinking about you. Not thinking about you really, just you were in my head. Right? Am I right? Or am I wrong?" He attempted to keep his thoughts rational, but what was in his head wasn't exactly coming out of his mouth in any kind of coherent fashion.

Dylan's tone softened. "It's nearly midnight on Christmas Eve, Mitch, why are you phoning me?"

There was whispering, something about drunk dialing, although the words were muffled. Mitch should have known the L-man would be there. "Dylan! My man, you still there?"

Dylan came back. "Mitch, Merry Christmas and all, but you gotta phone me after January first, man."

13

Oh yeah. After Christmas, and not on Christmas Eve. He felt a hysterical bubble of laughter in his throat. "Oh. My bad." Then he pressed on with the question he wanted answered. "So can I have your island?"

"Lucas can check dates after New Year's for you."

Lucas! That was his name. Not Liam or Luke. Lucas. "Lucas. How is he? Still the love of your life?" Mitch was genuinely happy for Dylan being happy. Well, sometimes he was happy for him. Other times he regretted having had a stick up his ass and never talking to Dylan about how he felt way back when. Never mind, that was in the past now.

"Goodbye, Mitch," Dylan said. The message was clear. *I have things to do on Christmas Eve and they don't include talking to you, Mitch.*

"Oh, okay then. Merry Christmas." The finality of the call ending, of losing a friendly voice on the phone, hit him, and suddenly he didn't feel so much drunk as tired.

"Hang on. Mitch, what are you doing for Christmas?"

Mitch considered what he was doing. Staying here overnight, eating the overpriced breakfast, drinking champagne, going home. "Nothing special."

"You seeing Dad?"

Regret slid through Mitch. There wasn't a single day when he didn't think about the final day working for Dylan's dad and Dylan himself. Still, he wasn't going to let Dylan know what he was feeling. Instead he cased the words in an icy disdain. "I don't work for him anymore. Couldn't. Not after he got all soft on a client and refused to seal the deal. We argued, I walked. Didn't he tell you?"

"We don't talk much," Dylan said after a pause. Then he changed the subject. "What about spending Christmas with your brother?"

My brother? With his wife and his picture-perfect house and his medical degree? That isn't happening this side of ever.

"He's in England with his new wife." Mitch began to feel defensive. Who was Dylan to think he could comment on Mitch's life? "I don't want to see anyone at Christmas." He snorted a laugh. "Jeez, Dylan, you getting slow in your old age playing house with that man of yours? We're not all settled down. Some of us like to play the field and enjoy ourselves."

"Uh-huh." Dylan didn't call him on his bullshit response. It was a good thing, because if Dylan continued in that direction, Mitch might fold under the strain. "Phone me in the New Year. And have a good Christmas, Mitch."

"You too," Mitch offered lamely. He ended the call and placed the cell carefully on the small side table. Then he tilted his head back to stare at the ceiling. *You too, Dylan.*

The pity-party-for-one lasted a good half hour, enough for the whiskey edge to fade, and he cursed himself for his stupidity. What was he doing sitting in his goddamned hotel room this early on Christmas Eve when he could be downstairs finding one of the favors and celebrating Christmas the way he should? *Maybe that brunet from the balcony, the one who looked barely legal with the dark eyes and the kiss-me lips.*

He used the bathroom, brushed his teeth, checked his hair, and donning his jacket, he left the room. When the elevator doors opened, he slid in and checked himself in the three walls of mirrors. He looked good for thirty-one. The elevator stopped at the eighteenth floor, and as if the fates were smiling on him, the guy from the balcony walked in, adjusting his shirt as he did. *Clearly on his way back from a meet-up.* He looked at Mitch warily.

"Sorry about earlier," Mitch said. Then, as the doors of the elevator slid shut, he pressed the escort against the glass and kissed him.

By the time the elevator reached the first floor, and hell, it must have only been a couple seconds, Mitch was hard and his hookup was wrapped around him like a monkey on a tree.

Mitch pressed the button to take them back up to his room. That decision was an easy one.

Mitch backed him out of the elevator and to his room, still kissing, still hard, and even when the door shut behind them, Mitch didn't stop kissing. They separated as they stumbled over Mitch's discarded shoes, and the young guy opened his mouth to speak.

"I'm—"

"No names needed," Mitch said firmly.

The man's eyes widened, but Mitch didn't give him a chance to form a reply, pushing him back until he lay on the bed, a wide grin on the escort's face.

"I can go with that," the escort said. He arched up as he shimmied out of slim pants and his pristine white shirt. "Not calling you anything," he added and curled up to pull at his socks. Finally, he lay in just leave-nothing-to-the-imagination briefs. He was already hard, but he didn't touch himself. Instead he sprawled back, his legs spread and his hands over his head and clasped together. He looked like he was fucking posing, all perfect hair and toned form.

Mitch shoved at his own clothes, and finally naked, he crawled up the bed and decided the best way to enjoy this gorgeous Christmas gift was to mess that perfection right up. He spent time kissing, enjoying the taste of whiskey and the promise of that mouth on his cock later. At the same time, he tousled the guy's hair with his fingers, finally pulling it free from the confines of gel and mousse and whatever the hell else was in it to keep it looking so damn designer. Finally he was happy and nuzzled his face into the man's neck, inhaling the scent there, citrus and spice and all things edible.

From there Mitch nipped and kissed a path to two perfect nipples in a hairless chest, loving the sensation of his lips on acres of smooth skin. One thing about the escorts, they were certainly high-class.

Traveling south, he pulled back the cotton to expose his bedmate's cock, hard and flushed with need, and only a sudden sense of self-preservation had him stopping.

"Where are your condoms?" Mitch asked and looked down at discarded pants.

"Shit. Don't have any," was the frustrated answer.

"What kind of a... never mind." Mitch wasn't thinking about why an escort would have run out of condoms already. Instead he was too needy, too tired of waiting around, and he rolled off the guy with haste. Rummaging in his wash bag, he grabbed condoms and his ever-present lube and was back on the bed before his lover decided to make a run for it. Given the wide-eyed expression on his face, it looked possible.

"I don't get —"

"Shh," Mitch said.

He slicked his fingers and slid them to the man's ass, pressing inside him with a sharp movement.

"Fuck," his one-night stand cursed.

Mitch stilled. For running out of condoms, this guy sure was tight. Jeez, was this guy a top? He'd never even thought to ask. When the escort screwed himself down onto Mitch's fingers and inhaled sharply before doing it again, Mitch decided he must be versatile. *Fucking thank God for that.*

Mitch stretched him, kissing the guy's inner thighs, before rolling on a condom and encouraging the escort onto all fours. Sinking into the tight heat was bliss; stilling his movement when the guy under him groaned was instinct.

"You okay?" he asked. Mitch might well be the third or fourth guy with this escort tonight, but he wasn't going to hurt him. Even though it went against every instinct he had, he stopped and waited. Finally his lover pushed back, and from there, everything was a blur.

Mitch closed his eyes and fucked every ounce of his need into this willing body. Falling back to his heels, he pulled the escort with him, every muscle in his body screaming for release. They kissed, awkwardly, messily at that angle, and Mitch opened his eyes, caught in the unfathomable brown of the escort's gaze. There was innocence there, lust, need. Mitch reached around as they kissed, and with a few twists the escort was coming, with Mitch not long after.

They fell to the bed in a tangle of limbs, the escort chuckling. "Fuck, that was hot."

"Mmm," Mitch hummed. He eased out and discarded the condom, wiping himself with tissues next to the bed. He passed the box to the other man and watched as he cleaned himself up.

Then with a contented smile, the escort closed his sexy, heavy-lidded dark eyes and in seconds was asleep.

Mitch reached over to shake him awake but stopped at the last moment. He looked so peaceful, all fucked out and sprawled on the bed. What the hell. It was a huge bed, and Mitch could stand to have a companion for a little while. He eased up from the bed, and just because he was a careful kind of guy, he locked his wallet in the small room safe.

After all, this guy might be a high-class escort, but he was still on the shady side. Finally, Mitch was back under the covers, and he closed his eyes, every muscle in his body relaxing.

* * * * *

When they woke and the escort used his talent to bring Mitch off with lips and hands only it was one hell of a way to be woken up. And when the man smiled up at him, his lips swollen and his expression heavy with lust, Mitch wished for a brief moment that this escort was just a normal guy. Because they were dynamite in bed.

They showered at some ungodly hour and that ended with Mitch fucking his hookup over the bathtub.

He woke at a little after six, only an hour before the shuttle was picking him up to take him home. He reached to nudge the escort awake. Then he stopped. The kid looked exhausted and sweet and vulnerable. Mitch shook the thoughts from his head, that insistent press that maybe he could do some kind of Richard Gere and get this guy into proper work. Not that being an escort was like hanging around on street corners, but there was something about his hookup that screamed connection.

What the hell am I looking for? Did he imagine he could sweep in and keep this one for real, like a Christmas story or something where he could give the young man a happy ending? Like an escort would give up the thousands he probably earned doing something he enjoyed for a chance with a bitter marketing exec.

Getting soft in my old age.

Instead of worrying any more, he left a tip on the small table and exited the room. The guy had been good, and that was a plus from an otherwise boring Christmas event.

Chapter 3

"Okay, okay." Mitch clutched his cell phone to his ear and deftly maneuvered between people. He winced as he swerved, narrowly missing taking a small child's head off with his bulky flight bag and instead running over the boy's foot with his case. He flashed a smile of apology to the boy's mother and kept moving.

"Mitch, are you listening to me?"

Mitch withheld an irritated sigh. "Send the files over to their office. They wanted it done for February first and that is today, so they can't complain, and I can't do anything until they've signed off on everything."

As Doris answered, he checked over his shoulder to make sure he hadn't lost his companion during the mad dash through the building.

"No. I don't know where that is, and there's nothing I can do about it now, is there?" He stopped abruptly and grunted as the man he was with walked into him. He glanced sideways at the photographer as Doris asked questions that he was too far away to do anything about. "I'm not going to remember this. I just got off a plane. I'm hot." *I may also be drunk.* He never had been much of a flier, and Dutch courage had turned into three or four drinks before they'd even taken off. "Email me, yeah? And I'll get back to you."

When he'd agreed to cover Jerry's job if Melinda went into labor, he hadn't actually expected to be here. He'd handed over details of Dylan's island and thought that would be the end of it. Then Melinda had fallen ill with preeclampsia, the baby had arrived eight weeks early, and suddenly Mitch had been thrust into working this location with very little information. Thank goodness both Melinda and baby were okay. The baby was in NICU, but the prognosis was good — that was the only positive from the whole situation. That and the fact Mitch got to see Dylan again.

The photographer fidgeted beside him. The skinny man with bright red-dyed hair had boyish good looks. He looked like he was barely out of his teens — Mitch wasn't convinced the man had even hit puberty, let alone had time to become people were touting as the next big thing, one of the best in the business. A year ago, Bruno Cash — real name — had been just another nobody with a camera. One Beyoncé photo shoot later, and the twenty-two-year-old had magazines and advertising companies throwing money at him like it was going out of fashion.

"Email me," Mitch repeated more slowly before hanging up. "Sorry." He turned to Bruno and took a breath. His focus should be here and not back in Miami. "Right, who are we looking for again?" He'd gotten the call from Jerry five days ago, and since then he'd been running around like an idiot playing catchup.

"Someone named Scott." Bruno pulled at the low neck of the baggy t-shirt he wore, then wiped his hand on the back of his faded and frayed jeans.

Mitch fingered the neat knot of his blue tie. He could only imagine what a mismatched pair they looked like right now. He smoothed his hand over the rich silk until he met the closed button of his gray jacket. Unfastening the button, he allowed the recent tension caused by the phone call to ebb away. The thought of seeing Dylan again made him nervous. Once he saw his ex he could figure out exactly what he was so nervous about and what the hell he was going to do about it.

The last time he'd seen Dylan was almost three years ago, when Dylan Senior had sent him to get Dylan's signature on a trust fund that was due to transfer to him. There had been almost a million dollars in the trust, and what had Dylan done with it? Bought himself a damn island. It had certainly been a surprising investment, but then Dylan had always been full of surprises.

"I think that's him," Bruno said and pointed to where two men were standing. One of the men held a sign with Mitch's full name handwritten on it.

Mitchell Travis Cartwright Stone. Mitch snorted a laugh. Trust Dylan to remember. He had hated his second middle name ever since some boy at school had taken it upon himself to nickname him Bonanza. The show had been canceled before he was even born, but with countless repeats, made-for-TV movies, and his classmate's obsession with westerns, the name had somehow stuck throughout high school.

With Bruno in tow, Mitch walked up to the men. "Scott?" He looked at the man holding the sign, who gave a short nod. Mitch was a little disappointed Dylan wasn't picking him up, but Scott wasn't all that bad a consolation prize. Scott was muscular, tanned, with dark hair and eyes similar to Dylan's, all sea green-blue.

"Would you like me to take anything?" asked the man standing next to Scott. He was slimmer than Scott, his jaw covered in a few days' growth, but the sun had blessed him with the same healthy glow. The man held out his hand and quirked an eyebrow. Apparently, he was aware of Mitch's lingering gaze on Scott.

"Thanks," Mitch said and handed over his flight bag. He rested his hand on Bruno's shoulder. "This is Bruno Cash. He's the photographer."

Bruno gave a small smile. He clutched his bag to his chest as he extended his hand.

Scott took Bruno's hand and smiled brightly. "I'm Scott, and this is Adam. Adam is the Cay's resident chef."

"And Scott's boyfriend," Adam added, clearly for Mitch's benefit.

There was a beat, and then Scott knitted his eyebrows together, obviously amused by the bold statement made by Adam. "Yeah. Anyway." Scott looked at Mitch. "Adam came along to make sure we had everything based on the list of dietary requirements you sent through for you and your team."

Well, that was one item Mitch could tick off his to-do list. "Excellent."

Adam looked like he wanted to say something, but Scott interrupted. "Seriously, if he starts talking about produce and prime cuts, he'll be at it all night." Scott winked at Adam, who feigned annoyance before grinning.

"Do you want me to take anything else?"

"I think we're good," Mitch answered for himself and Bruno.

"Then *Lady Liberty* awaits."

Mitch nodded toward the exit. "Lead the way."

* * * * *

Please make it stop.

Mitch breathed through his nose as he hugged the side of the boat. Apparently, he couldn't fly *or* travel by boat.

"They say keep your eyes on the horizon," Scott chimed from the front of the boat. He glanced at Mitch over the top of his sunglasses.

"Yeah, thanks," Mitch said gruffly. He checked the horizon, finding nothing more than a mass of blue as the ocean met the sky. Closing his eyes, he took deep breaths. He was just grateful he'd only had a liquid breakfast. At the thought of breakfast, he gagged and pressed his hand to his mouth. He curled his fingers against his jaw and willed the feeling away. Surely he had nothing left in his stomach.

"Ten minutes," Scott called to him and Bruno.

Mitch simply nodded, daring to lower his hand and take a sip from the bottled water Adam had handed to him. He needed something to focus on, and he didn't mean the horizon. Swallowing back the urge to vomit for a fourth time, Mitch ran through what he could remember from his checklist.

He had all the emails that Jerry had been exchanging with the clothing company and Lucas prior to it landing it Mitch's lap. And he'd actually needed to email Lucas quite a lot since taking over from Jerry in the last week. At first, part of him wished it was Dylan doing the contacting, but he had eventually figured it was for the best.

The boat tilted in the water, and cool, salty spray hit his face. He felt like crap. He was hot, sweating like hell in his suit, and could only imagine how pale and disgusting he looked right now as he grasped desperately at the side of the boat.

Oh God.

His mind had wandered and he tried to get back to his original focus, his list. There were hotel rooms to check over, he needed to arrange security and storage for equipment on the Cay, and then confirm flight arrival details for the rest of the team. It included six models, their entourage for hair, makeup, and outfits, and a handful of other people setting up the shots and props. He also had the last-minute addition of the company owner's son, who was overlooking the whole thing and apparently used to be a model. *So, a pretty-boy airhead*, Mitch figured.

They were all due to arrive on the island in two days' time. Then there were locations to scout out with Bruno and a schedule to keep everyone to. At least it seemed this Adam had a handle on the dietary requirements for the models and crew, including a couple of vegetarians, a shellfish allergy, and one female model intolerant to gluten. And then Mitch still had to find the time to talk to Dylan. It wasn't really about looking for a way back in, not anymore. He just wanted to wish Dylan good luck. Any thoughts of Dylan throwing over Lucas and flinging himself at Mitch had long gone. Well, not *long* gone, just since Christmas Eve night. When unexpectedly, he had shared a connection with someone who wasn't Dylan, and no matter how brief it might have been, it had been real. It was enough for Mitch to realize it could just as easily happen again with someone else. Dylan had moved on and maybe it was time he did too.

"Are you okay?" Bruno asked and rested his hand on Mitch's shoulder.

Mitch briefly opened his eyes and glanced at Bruno. The photographer looked a little pale himself. "Mmm," Mitch mumbled and lowered his head. He rested his forehead against the back of his hand.

"My girlfriend can't ride a bus without getting sick. She takes Dramamine. Do you not have anything like that?"

"No," Mitch said bluntly. Maybe if he'd known he was going to be like this, he could have prepared himself.

"Right."

"Sorry." Slowly, Mitch sat up. "I don't do sick very well."

Bruno smiled. "No worries." He stared toward the front of the boat. "Have you seen it?"

"What?"

"The island." Bruno pointed. "It's really something, huh? A whole island to ourselves for ten days."

Mitch considered the island as they moved closer. The white sands were stunning against the dark backdrop of foliage, and half-hidden by the trees, the hotel was at the highest point of the island.

"It is," Mitch agreed.

* * * * *

Never had Mitch been happier than when he set his feet on the solidly built pier. He resisted the urge to fall to his knees and kiss the wooden beams, still a bit shaky like he was still on the damn boat. Then his head settled, and he took a moment to enjoy the feel of… well, nothing. No more swaying, no more motion, just standing very, very still.

Where the pier met the sand, Dylan was standing with a second man Mitch recognized from an online wedding magazine article as Lucas. He thought it was fair to say Dylan had a type and that type was good-looking blonds, if he said so himself.

"Mitch," Dylan greeted him as he and Bruno reached the end of the pier.

"D," Mitch said.

Dylan was unfazed by the old nickname. "How was your flight?"

"On time," Mitch said and laughed. He'd been glad to get off the plane, and now he was equally, if not more so, happy to be off the damn boat.

"This is Lucas." Dylan waved a hand toward Lucas, who smiled politely. Sunlight caught the ring on Dylan's finger as he added, "My fiancé."

"I heard," Mitch said. "Congratulations." He held his hand out to Lucas, who took it easily. Lucas's grip was strong as he gave Mitch's hand a firm shake. "It's nice to finally meet you."

"You too," Lucas said as he lowered his hand. "It's good to be able to put a face to the name."

Mitch wasn't sure what to say. "That sounds ominous," he joked. What had Dylan said about him?

Dylan smirked. Was he enjoying this? "Don't worry. It wasn't all bad." Dylan gave nothing away as he spoke. "Anyway, I'm going to help the boys unload. Lucas will show you and…"

"Bruno," Bruno said. He made a move to offer his hand but gave up, having reclaimed all of his luggage already and with no actual free hand to use.

"And Bruno to your rooms. We'll meet up for a late lunch in a couple of hours. Give you both time to settle in and grab a shower and change." He looked at Mitch. "We can talk itinerary and if there's anything else you need from us."

"Thanks," Bruno answered. "It would be great to hear your ideas for locations, natural features of the island, and lighting."

Dylan nodded. "We can do that. We'll talk later." He went to leave, but not before a show of affection toward his man.

As Dylan leaned in and kissed Lucas on the cheek, Mitch averted his eyes. Mitch knew Lucas was watching him, scrutinizing his every word and move around Dylan, *his* fiancé. Maybe Lucas was right to do that, Mitch thought, as a pang of jealousy reared its head. The emotion quickly faded, though. Mitch was glad, because it meant he'd been right. Right about moving on.

Lucas waited, obvious in his watching of Dylan as he made his way back along the pier to join Scott and Adam in unloading the boat. Seemingly content, he then turned his attention to his guests, smiled brightly, and said, "Welcome to Sapphire Cay."

Chapter 4

Robert Bailey frowned at Isaac. "Are you sure you can handle this? I wish I was going with you. We could drive. Just because I can't fly doesn't mean we couldn't get in the car, drive down, and then take a ferry to the Cays."

Isaac sighed internally. This wasn't the first time his dad had doubted him and it wouldn't be the last. He couldn't let his dad see that he was getting more and more wound up by the constant questions. Last night his dad had called three times. The first time had just been to organize a gift for Isaac's mom's birthday, but the second one had morphed into a 'this is important' speech.

"And how will you manage if you get sick on the island?" Isaac asked. His dad was not long getting over a gall bladder operation, and he had a follow-up operation in a couple weeks.

"We could take a nurse."

Isaac looked at his dad pointedly. Robert Bailey would need to start to think rationally to have any chance of winning this conversation. Isaac knew this shoot was important. He was fully aware of how much Bailey's Clothing had invested in this new line of designs. Moving up from franchises in larger department stores to having their own shops in two major cities was a big step, and it was all riding on Isaac's growing notoriety as a designer worth watching.

When the third call had been his dad near-hyperventilating at the list of things that could go wrong, Isaac had known he had to do something. He'd told his dad to go to bed and that they'd talk in the morning before he left for his flight. Now, with his dad pacing the large air-conditioned office and muttering about budgets, Isaac simply leaned back against the corner of his drafting table, the one he'd been riding since last summer, and crossed his arms over his chest.

"I know what we're doing, Dad. This was my idea, right? I have the details in my head backed up with notes, and procedures and schedules coming out my ass. Yes, I can handle this."

His dad sighed audibly, "Look, I know I was only twenty-two when I started Bailey's, but I wasn't like you." His dad stopped, the big bear of a man going scarlet as he realized what he had said.

"Like me," Isaac repeated softly. "An ex-model? Gay? Young? Skinny? What? I'm twenty-six and I

Capture the Sun

have a degree in business, Dad, and these are my designs, my work."

"I'd feel better if we'd managed to get Jerry to carry on working with you."

"Well, his wife having the baby two months early kind of got in the way of that, didn't it?" Isaac said tiredly.

"I know Jerry referred us to this new guy, but he's a troubleshooter, not a project manager."

"Apparently he has all the right stuff for what we need. And for whatever reason, he's made himself available to join us." Isaac pushed himself away from the desk and picked up his carry-on bag. Inside he had his laptop, with his design software backed up, and he had an hour after check-in to look over final design briefs. The wardrobe of clothes, from formal to underwear, had already been dispatched to Sapphire Cay, but he had some last-minute thoughts on how to present the entire collection.

"I'd feel better if you'd actually managed to talk to the man before you got to the shoot."

"Jerry passed on everything I need." Isaac didn't mention that he too wished that he had met this Mitchell guy in a more formal setting, but at least Mitchell had agreed to accompany the whole

37

entourage to the island to liaise with Isaac and the island staff. That was a good thing.

Isaac hadn't expected that—he'd imagined it would just be him organizing this shoot—but he was grateful for any support. Glancing at his watch, he realized he really needed to get a move on. He'd booked the car for ten and it was nine fifty already. He crossed to his dad and hugged him close.

"I'll call and email every day."

"See that you do," his dad blustered even as he hugged Isaac. Then, as if he recalled his place in the whole father-son dynamic, he extended the hug. "Good luck, Isaac. I'm sorry to worry. I know you'll do well."

* * * * *

Only after he'd had a drink and was settled back in the plane seat did the doubts he'd hidden from his dad rise to the surface. He allowed himself to panic for ten minutes, even listed every single thing that could go wrong, from a boat-sinking tragedy to a hurricane. Then he forcibly stopped himself.

He was Isaac Bailey, and as much as everyone looked at him like he was a kid and an ex-model with no brains, he had a degree in business. Not only that, but he had grown up in the world of fashion, following his dad everywhere. He wasn't going to fuck this up, and they wouldn't lose money.

If all else failed, he could always have more random sex like he'd had Christmas Eve, because evidently falling into bed with a stranger while drunk paid well. He'd tried to think of a better explanation, but based on the kind of party they'd been at, there was only one real answer for the bills on the nightstand. The hot-as-fuck man had thought Isaac was an escort.

He huffed to himself. Yes, at least if he did fuck this week up, there was always another line of work he could venture into.

* * * * *

The chaos at the dock was exciting. With his carry-on over his shoulder and tugging his suitcase behind him, he was in the middle of a group of seriously hot models, and heads were turning. The wolf-whistles were a rush, but just as he had been when he was a model himself at sixteen, he was shy at the thought of anyone looking at him. Which of course they weren't, because, let's face it, the six models alongside him were gorgeous.

Although…

Not as gorgeous as one Scott-from-Sapphire-Cay, who was helping each of them into a boat called the *Lady Liberty*. Now *he* was something to look at. Not model-slim and waiflike, no makeup or carefully teased hair. Scott was all golden-tanned… yum. Unfortunately, so was the boyfriend who was waiting for him at the dock on Sapphire Cay.

Isaac envied the easy hugs and quick kiss and the bantering as the two men helped models alight and paired each one up with luggage that had come over on the previous boat. Must be nice to have that camaraderie, that obvious love, and the PDAs were seriously hot.

"Hi, I'm Dylan Gray. Welcome to Sapphire Cay." A man in cutoffs, with brown hair shot through with blond and skin the color of burnished copper, offered a hand, and Isaac shook it firmly.

"Your island is beautiful."

Dylan smiled, and there were honest-to-God dimples, pits of cute. Hell, was everyone on this island all-natural and gorgeous?

40

"We'll get everyone settled in, and then if you're up to it, there are cocktails at the pool bar for you to meet everyone. Kind of a welcome thing."

Cocktails? In this beautiful place? That sounded like paradise.

Dylan and Isaac exchanged small talk while the models organized themselves, and finally all of them were shown to their rooms in the main hotel. He wondered where Bruno Cash might be. He couldn't wait to catch up with the photographer. He loved Bruno's work and it was a coup to get him to agree to shoot for this layout.

* * * * *

Isaac got a shower, changed into a pair of his own-design board shorts, a clash of scarlet and green, and went outside to find the pool. He'd lathered on sun block again like he had this morning. His fair skin had a tendency to burn at the slightest amount of sun. It was kind of ironic given he lived in the Sunshine State.

He detoured to the beach and pulled off his beach shoes before wriggling his toes in the hot sand. Stretching tall and yawning as today caught up with him, he took his time to look around at the

41

parts of the island he could see. What he had originally viewed from his seat on the *Liberty* was even more stunning close up. His artist's eye saw a beautiful hotel set back into trees at the top of the island, white sand, and sea the color of the tie that the stranger had worn at Christmas.

Fuck. There it is again.

The stranger at the party came back into his thoughts at the strangest times. He had to have been a guest or something, but a perverse part of Isaac kept him from tracking the guy down. Yes, they'd been good in bed — and over the bath and in the shower and on the bed again — but the guy had vanished without even a goodbye. What kind of man did that? No one Isaac wanted permanent with, obviously.

Someone who was drunk. Evidently.

"Hi," a voice said to his left. "Bruno Cash."

Isaac turned to face the man who held the job of making Bailey's fashions look good. He was skinny with bright red-dyed hair and didn't look much older than eighteen, even though Isaac knew Bruno was only four years younger than him. He felt an instant camaraderie, and instead of shaking hands, they hugged.

"It's cool to finally meet you," Isaac offered.

"Yeah, sorry about that, but London was calling, and I had to prioritize," Bruno said with a shrug. Then he was straight down to business. "I looked over your portfolio. You want a rugged feel to the photo shoot, I get that."

Isaac nodded and they chatted as they made their way toward the pool, completely oblivious to anything but the imaginings of two creative minds.

"And I'm thinking red," Bruno said, "as a theme."

"Yes," Isaac replied with equal enthusiasm. "Sunset, sunrise, but dulled down, like rusts, perfect."

In a flurry of hugs the two men formed a friendship based on scarlet and fashion. Isaac hoped things went as well when they started shooting.

They were still laughing and chatting when they ended up at the bar, although Bruno wandered off, saying he was calling his girlfriend. Scott-from-the-boat was behind the wooden bar, shaking a startlingly green drink for someone who had his back to him. When he poured it out, he added pineapple from a large dish and a fluorescent lemon umbrella. Isaac didn't care what it was, he wanted the same.

"I'll have what he's having," he said on a laugh.

The man on the seat swiveled to face him and every sound of laughter died in a split second.

Isaac would recognize those clear blue eyes anywhere.

For a second Isaac was absolutely silent, and he was aware of the weight of the stranger's stare at him. The stranger looked from him to Bruno and back again with a hint of mockery in the depth of his gaze.

Isaac ignored the surprise that still thrummed through his body and extended his hand.

"I think I owe you a couple hundred dollars," he quipped.

Blue eyes leaned forward. "It was a tip," he said so that only Isaac could hear.

The bottom fell out of Isaac's normally sunny world. A tip? For what? For the frankly awesome sex? Then he sighed inwardly. He'd been right: this guy *had* thought him an escort, just as Isaac had suspected when he'd woken to an empty room, no sign of his new lover, and a pile of twenties. Add in the whole no-name thing, and he'd realized in the cold light of day that he'd been mistaken for one of the party favors. *What the hell?* Embarrassment flooded him with the confirmation, but he

44

resolutely did not move his hand, still extended in welcome.

Cosmic karma had landed the stranger from one night of sex in his lap. And that stranger looked a mix of surprised and horrified.

Well, funnily enough, the man didn't have the sole right to either of those. In the space of a few seconds, a sexy liaison at a party had become something sordid wherein Isaac had been tipped for the night. Tipped!

"Isaac Bailey," he introduced himself.

Recognition showed on the stranger's face. Sudden, shocked recognition. Finally he shook Isaac's proffered hand.

"Mitchell Stone," he said.

Before Isaac could extend the conversation, Mitchell slid off the stool, muttered something under his breath, and stalked off to the hotel. Isaac made to follow, but someone held his arm. When he looked it was one of the models, a slinky brunette with curves in all the right places for his designs.

She pouted, "Come swim."

Isaac considered her perfect makeup and hoped to hell it was waterproof; otherwise, when it slid down her face, it would look a mess. He didn't think she would like that very much. Her insistence on a swim had stopped him from doing something really stupid. Like running after Mitchell and…

And what? Pushing him to the sand and kissing him? Shouting at him? Demanding he take back the money? Or what?

"Later," he said to the model. He needed thinking time. Too much was riding on this shoot, and the last thing he needed to do was lose focus.

"You okay? Do you know Mitch?" Scott passed over a green fruity drink.

"Briefly." He decided he didn't need thinking time at all. What he needed was drinking time.

Starting now.

Chapter 5

Well, this was fucking great. Under his breath Mitch cursed Jerry and this job. It had to be some kind of joke. The universe was having a laugh at his expense.

God, if you're listening, please just let the ground open up now.

This was so embarrassing and so unprofessional. Dylan Senior had imparted plenty of advice during Mitch's years working for him, one such gem being *Don't sleep with the clients.* He could hear the old man's voice now. Mitch had messed up big time. Quickly, he made his way around the side of the hotel before coming to a halt. He'd left a tip. A fucking tip.

Taking a deep breath, he leaned back against the side of the building. He remembered back to Christmas Eve and the assumptions he'd made based on nothing more than a guy being polite at a party. What world did Mitch inhabit where judging a man on a simple moment was okay? Was he that jaded?

Laughter echoed from the back of the hotel as the models and crew bonded over cocktails. Mitch looked back along the path he'd walked and was relieved no one had followed him. He had no idea what he was going to say to the Bailey kid. Sure, the company was small in comparison to the Davis/Haddison-Walker contracts he'd worked on, but they all moved in the same circles. One misplaced comment and what might have been an amusing anecdote for most could be a career-ender for him. He'd slept with the son of Robert Bailey, the man paying his wage, and left cash thinking the kid was a hooker.

Don't be so melodramatic. He closed his eyes and rested back his head. *Cool it, Mitch.*

Thinking ten steps ahead was what Mitch was good at. Very rarely had he been caught off guard in all his years of setting up contracts and negotiating bonuses. He planned all the possible twists and turns to get the outcome he wanted. But this he hadn't planned for, and his current train of thought started with him messing up this job and ended with him absconding to Alaska.

Chiding himself, he shook his head and pushed off the wall. He should probably talk to Isaac before declaring his career dead and buried. Besides, the way he saw it, Isaac wouldn't want anyone knowing he'd been mistaken for a hooker, because what did that say about him? Mitch relaxed as he thought more rationally about the situation. Isaac wouldn't want to make this common knowledge either. Not if he valued his career in fashion design. He already had his ex-model image to contend with. Being mistaken for an escort would just add to his airhead persona.

A twinge of guilt spread outward from Mitch's stomach, and the taste of the green cocktail fizzed at the back of his throat. His emotions were conflicted as he remembered back to Christmas Eve and their time together at the hotel. He'd had fun, was pretty damn sure Isaac had too. There hadn't been many words that night, their bodies doing the talking as they'd fucked into the early hours. Mitch remembered Isaac's flawless skin, paler than the usual tanned beauties on show in Miami, the thick dark waves of his hair.

Blinking, he turned as voices neared. He needed to talk to someone about this, but not models or crew, and certainly not Isaac. Not yet.

I need to talk to Dylan.

Head down, he walked around to the front of the hotel. He'd been on the island for a couple of days, preferring to spend his time replying to emails in his room or accompanying Bruno on his exploration of the island. Mitch had always thought he had a good eye, but he had been impressed with the young photographer. Bruno had gone out at all hours of the day checking on lighting and angles. He'd walked the beaches, hunted for props and suitable backgrounds, and ventured away from the neat and trimmed gardens, through the undergrowth and low-hanging trees in search of something secluded and special. Seemed he'd found it when he came back raving about some shack and a spring.

Mitch slipped inside the hotel and decided to try Dylan's office first. Apart from the muted sound of people outside by the pool, the hotel was eerily quiet. The afternoon sun flooded through the doors leading out to the patio, lighting the empty entrance. There was no one else around. Mitch stopped when he heard voices. He could make out Dylan and Lucas as they talked.

"I don't think he likes me," Lucas said. There was the sound of a chair creaking.

"Don't be stupid," Dylan replied. "There's nothing not to like."

"He's hardly said two words to me the whole time he's been here."

"And I'm sure you've gone out of your way to speak to him." Dylan had laughter in his tone.

They were obviously talking about him. It wasn't like Mitch was purposely avoiding Lucas. He just didn't know what to say. Maybe if Lucas still worked in the business world, they'd have something other than Dylan in common. As it was, he didn't think comparing notes on their relationships with Dylan was on either of their to-do lists.

Lucas was silent, but there was the sound of movement as one of the men, Mitch assumed Dylan, crossed the room to join the other.

"You know me and him are—"

Lucas interrupted. "I know there's nothing there. Not anymore. I just…"

"What?"

"Does he know it?"

The pair fell silent, and Mitch dared to lean forward, catching a glimpse of the couple around the edge of the door. Lucas was sitting on the desk, and Dylan standing between his legs, kissing him. Mitch couldn't help but smile as he watched. They looked happy and in love.

Good for you, Dylan.

The kiss ended and Mitch moved back.

"Okay?" Dylan asked.

"Yeah."

"Good. Now, about Edward, he called to ask us questions, but I said we'd need to talk first."

"What you mean to say is that with less than four weeks to go until our big day, you're scared of our wedding planner."

Mitch felt the tug in his chest at the words. Wedding. He'd known they were engaged, but an actual wedding? That soon? Seeing Dylan settled in one place was one thing, but to hear him and Lucas talking weddings was another. Mitch realized he was just a little bit jealous.

"Well, yeah, but it's only fair," Dylan teased. "Connor French left a message about deciding he'd like to visit the island, and I'm handling that one."

"When are you saying he should visit? And did he say anything about knowing who Alfie was?"

"No, he doesn't, and I said the quiet week before the wedding."

"You think it will be quiet?"

"It will be for me," Dylan said. "I'll be hiding in a closet somewhere."

More kissing and laughing, and Mitch began to edge away. He'd heard enough.

"Okay, we can work something. I'll call Edward."

"I'm going to check on our guests," Dylan said. He leaned in and kissed Lucas on the forehead. "Tell Edward I said hi." He headed for the door.

Shit. Mitch winced, turning to run. He didn't get far before Dylan said his name in a puzzled tone. "Mitch?"

Mitch looked over his shoulder. "Oh, hi. There you are." He slapped on a smile and looked past Dylan as Lucas stuck his head out of the office. Both men looked at him expectantly. "I just came to say... thanks for settling everybody in and for the cocktails." His words were stilted as he tried to think of a reason he was there that wouldn't give Lucas cause to hit him.

Neither man looked convinced — hell, Mitch wasn't convinced. Dylan glanced at Lucas and nodded.

"Hey, Mitch," Lucas said. "I need to..." He pointed into the office. "Do things. Later."

"Yeah." Mitch cleared his throat and turned on his heel. Surely he'd earned that hole to be sucked into now. This day was getting more awkward by the moment.

"Hey," Dylan called after him. "You okay?"

Mitch stopped and curled his hands into fists. He'd come looking for Dylan, and he'd definitely found him. What the hell, right? Spinning around, he met Dylan's eyes. Such a beautiful shade of blue. It was clear from the expression on Dylan's face that he was annoyed but interested in why Mitch was there.

"I wondered if we could talk."

Dylan looked back at the now-closed office door. "Sure," he agreed. "We can talk." He started walking and Mitch followed, surprised when they ended up in the kitchen.

"Adam, will you give us a minute?" Dylan said as Adam stood up after taking a tray of what looked like mini quiches out of the oven.

Adam turned the dials on the stove and nodded. "Sure. The timer goes off in ten." He wiped his hands on his apron and then pulled it up and over his head. "I'll go give Scott a hand."

"So," Dylan said once Adam was gone. "Are you going to start or shall I?"

"I had sex with Isaac Bailey on Christmas Eve," Mitch blurted out.

Dylan looked startled. Clearly, that was not what he had expected Mitch to say. "Okay?"

"We were at this party. I didn't know it was him. I thought he was—" He stopped. Dylan didn't need to know that. "Let's just say I made an idiot of myself."

A smile curled Dylan's lips.

Mitch sighed. "Yes, I know. I'm an idiot. Always have been." Damn if Dylan didn't have fucking dimples right now. "Anyway, that isn't what I really wanted to say. I wanted to say I was sorry."

"To Isaac?"

"To you." He pursed his lips. "And Isaac. But mostly you." There, that was what this was all about. Not Dylan himself, but Dylan's forgiveness. Mitch had messed up and had been no better than Dylan's father. Work had come first, and Dylan had deserved better. Dylan had *found* better in Lucas.

"So, yeah. I'm sorry. Sorry I was a selfish bastard who put work first when we were together." That felt good. Fuck if he didn't feel lighter.

Dylan shrugged. "It's fine. I get it. Your career was and is important to you. Just like Dad's."

"It shouldn't have been more important than you." Mitch leaned against the edge of the counter. "After everything you told me—your childhood, your dad. I know I let you down."

"It's fine. Some things just aren't meant to be." Dylan straightened up. "And I have Lucas now and we're getting married."

"Do you love him?"

Dylan nodded. "Very much."

"And he loves you?"

With a smile, Dylan said, "He does."

Folding his arms, Mitch returned Dylan's smile. "Good. Good. You deserve that." He lowered his eyes, his smile remaining as he was filled with a warmth and happiness for his old love. He could honestly say he was happy for Dylan.

"You do too."

Mitch shrugged. "Maybe." He briefly met Dylan's eyes. "Or maybe, like you said, some things aren't meant to be." He thought about Isaac. Things had been great that night when it had been about sex. Beyond that, however, he was sure he'd screw up eventually, assuming he hadn't already. That was what he did. Screw up.

There was something in Dylan's eyes when Mitch met his gaze, and it was clear Dylan didn't share

Mitch's belief that his messing up was inevitable. "I guess that's up to you," Dylan said.

"Is this where you give me the 'you work too hard and money can only bring you so much happiness' speech?"

"Would it make a difference if I did?"

Probably not. He chewed on his lip. Or could it? "Your dad seemed to think it might." A few grandkids via his girlfriend and a small hernia operation, and Dylan Senior had decided it was time to reevaluate his priorities. Mitch had gotten an entire speech about life being too short.

"What happened there?" Dylan asked. "With you and Dad, I mean."

Dylan's dad had always been about profit and, with Mitch at his side, had been out to get the best deal for them, for the company. "Have you ever seen *Pretty Woman*?"

"Yeah. A couple of times. Should I be admitting that?" Dylan laughed.

"Your dad was Richard Gere and his hernia was Julia Roberts." Mitch laughed, hoping it made sense. "He just lost his edge. He was no longer prepared to swoop in and get the best deal no matter what." He shrugged. "There was this one contract with Peters and Grant. They're a shipping company out of Charlotte. I'd worked damned hard on the contract. It was as good as signed. Turned out they had several ties with charitable organizations, made a lot of donations from profits instead of giving staff ridiculously sized bonuses, so your dad decided to settle for a smaller percentage to us so they didn't have to cut back on that."

Dylan's face brightened. There was a clear sense of pride in hearing what his dad had done.

"I lost it," Mitch began. "I know I probably sound like an asshole, but profit is our business. It's what we'd always done. I guess I didn't get what your dad was trying to do." He got it now. Mitch had scrolled through the list of past donations, many made to various cancer charities. Though the father-son relationship was strained, Dylan Senior loved his son, and Mitch knew the fear the old man had held for a long time concerning his son's health and all the nightmare scenarios. What if the cancer had taken him? What if they had to go through it all over again? "In the heat of the moment I walked away." He paused. Maybe he shouldn't have, but it was done. He'd walked away from the security of working for someone like Dylan Gray Senior and had started over somewhere new.

"You don't have to explain yourself to me," Dylan insisted. "I get what you and Dad used to do. Like you said, it's business."

Mitch nodded. "So, that's it really, and here I am."

"But you're okay, yeah?" Dylan examined his face, apparently examining for any telltale signs Mitch wasn't.

"I am," Mitch assured him. "I have to confess I was worried at first, but I'm actually okay. Great, in fact." The change had been good for him. A fresh challenge. A fresh start.

Dylan smiled. "So, what about Isaac? What are you going to do?"

Good question. "I'm the kind of person who thinks things through, right? I can do this." Mitch rubbed at his face. He told himself he needed to keep it professional even as the memory of Isaac naked and wanton came to the forefront of his mind. The thought had him hard, and he straightened up, thankful for his loose-fitting pants. Staying professional might be a harder task than he'd thought.

Mitch was startled as the timer went off on the oven.

Dylan pressed a button beneath a digital screen. Looking at Mitch, he said, "Time's up."

Mitch nodded. There was no point putting it off any longer. He'd talk to Isaac and work things out. They were both grownups, after all.

Chapter 6

Isaac dipped under the water again and held his breath for as long as he could. Set into the sides of the pool were intriguing shells and the water was still and clear. Also, being under the water meant Crystal, the model with the nails, wasn't able to get hold of him. There'd been far too much play-fighting involving her hands on him for his liking.

Could he be any more obviously gay? How did she even consider that he would be interested in her? Seemed to him being the boss's son made her think he'd be a useful upwardly mobile move.

When he had to break the surface, he swam to the side and heaved himself out before she had a chance to reach him. He didn't even look back; instead he grabbed a towel and chose the lounger next to Bruno. Tugging at it, he managed to get it mostly in the shade and, with a heartfelt sigh, lay back and stared up at the sky. Unbroken by clouds, it was the purest azure, as blue as Mitch's eyes.

Shame flooded him as he thought about Mitch again, and he shut his eyes tight. He'd been mistaken for a lot of things in his life, but never an escort. He'd been carded so many times he'd given up ordering alcohol at any bar he visited, and he'd had a couple of men come on to him because they thought he was underage. No one had ever decided to have sex with him because they thought it was on a plate for them. He groaned inwardly and crossed his arms over his eyes. How the hell was he going to look Mitch in the eyes without turning scarlet? Not to mention the fact that just seeing him had Isaac hardening in his pants. The memories of what they had done, of the highs he'd been taken to, were just too much to ignore.

He moved his hands to his sides, but couldn't bring himself to open his eyes in case someone decided to talk to him.

A shadow fell across him, and he was sure it was Crystal. "I'm freaking gay," he muttered.

Someone let out an embarrassed huff, and Isaac realized he was wrong. He opened his eyes and blinked up at Mitch, who stood uneasily next to him. "I should hope you are after what we did." He crouched down next to Isaac. "Look, can we talk?" he asked softly. He glanced around them, and Isaac followed his gaze. They were surrounded by people, staff, models, and Bruno was sitting not that far away. "I found this place, a garden..."

Isaac nodded and moved to set his feet flat on the floor. Then, in as smoothly as he could manage with a head rush, he stood with the towel held protectively in front of him. He wasn't hard but he was only in trunks, whereas Mitch was in a shirt and pants with a freaking tie. On an island. A tie.

Mitch turned and started walking and not once did he glance back to see if Isaac was following. It gave Isaac the chance to simply sit down again if he wanted. There was nothing written anywhere that said he had to talk about anything but business with Mitch. But over a week on an island trying to work with the man would likely be hard if they didn't at least clear the air.

He trailed after Mitch and thanked the heavens that Mitch had found a cool area where palm trees gave shade. Bright pink flowers crowded around them, giving them a sense of privacy. He could still hear the others by the pool, but it had been a convoluted walk to get to this place, and they weren't likely to be interrupted. Whatever they said here would be just between them.

Mitch turned to face Isaac, and his expression was a picture of shame.

"I spoke to Scott," he began. "He can take me back to the mainland tomorrow if that's what you would like." He said the words like it was the only reasonable option and Isaac would immediately agree.

Panic flared inside Isaac. He'd been counting on Jerry's replacement holding his hand with this whole thing so he could focus on his designs. Could someone else do it? Did Isaac actually want anyone else to do it?

"Don't be so fucking stupid," Isaac snapped. Where the irritation came from he wasn't entirely sure. Probably a mix of wanting to protect this shoot and his own embarrassment at some of the more erotic memories he had from Christmas. When Isaac looked at Mitch's lips, all he could recall was them wrapped around his cock or parted in ecstasy as he came.

Mitch's eyes widened comically. He obviously hadn't been expecting that. Suddenly, Isaac felt guilty. Mitch was only trying to do what he thought was the right thing, remove himself from the equation so that they wouldn't have to stare at each other and remember what had happened.

"I'm not being stupid," Mitch defended himself. "I apologize for what happened at Christmas. I can't blame the drink, but I stepped outside the boundaries by assuming things I shouldn't have."

"Like the fact I was a hooker," Isaac summarized.

"Shit, no, not a hooker. An escort." Mitch flushed red.

Isaac crossed his arms over his chest, and in doing so, the towel fell to the floor. He didn't care. Mitch had seen everything already anyway. Not that there was much to see now. Yes, he had been half-hard, but the fear that his manager would up and leave him on his first professional shoot was enough to knock his cock back down to size. Anyway, his board shorts were baggy. *Why am I even thinking about my dick?*

"There's a difference?" he finally said. Then he relaxed his stance and held up a hand. "Doesn't matter what you thought or what I thought or the money or whatever. I was there to enjoy myself that night, and I did. We had sex, you left, I put the two hundred in a can by a homeless guy on Fifth. End of story."

"Do you accept my apology?"

Isaac could see the apprehension in Mitch's face, like he hated the fact he was even having this conversation but knew that he had to.

"Fuck's sake," Isaac cursed. "What for? For the sex? For the blow jobs? And the fucking over the bath? And the amazing orgasms?"

"Jeez," Mitch said on a breath. He clenched his hands into fists at his sides. "You're doing this here?"

"What? You want me to gloss over what we did? Well, I'm not going to, because it was a fucking awesome night, and you treated me differently from any other guy I've been with. Like…"

"Like what?"

You didn't treat me like I'm a means to get close to my dad or an ex-model with no brains or rich or way too young. He'd dealt with those things more times than he cared to remember. No, Mitch had just treated him like a lover and played his body like an instrument, wringing orgasms out of him when Isaac thought he was done.

"Like I was a man," he finally said. Because that was true. The anonymity of the sex he'd had was the best part of it. The way Mitch had used him, dragged him to highs he'd never felt, the way they'd switched and for the first time ever, he had shown someone else what he could do. He'd been the one to drag Mitch to an orgasm so intense Mitch couldn't catch his breath and had sprawled for the longest time on the quilt cursing softly at what Isaac had done.

Mitch alternated between confused and disbelieving. "I don't understand."

Isaac huffed. "No one ever does." He recalled his last boyfriend, the non-conversations,

Capture the Sun

unreciprocated feelings, the fact the guy had pretty much used Isaac and seen him as one more ride on the way to a penthouse suite. "You had fun, and you're done. Look, I get that it's not going to happen again. We had fun, and now we're back to ex-model and businessman."

He turned his back on Mitch and made to leave their small secluded space but was yanked back hard. He let out a surprised yelp as Mitch twisted him and held him with a tight grip on his upper arms.

"You think that's it?" Mitch said harshly. "That we can just move back to normal after what we did?"

"Well, we have to." Isaac was confused. What else would they have? There was no point in hanging on to a yesterday when they had all the todays to worry about.

"You're in my head," Mitch snapped.

Isaac shook off Mitch's grip and stepped back. What did Mitch expect him to say to that? "It *was* a good night," he began tentatively.

"A good night." Mitch huffed and pressed at his temples, his jaw tensed. "You don't get it, do you? When we were together, I thought it was just one night, but when I left, I had this whole fucked-up idea in my head that I was Richard freaking Gere."

"Richard Gere?" Isaac was lost until sudden realization hit him. *Pretty Woman?* "You wanted to save me from my life of selling my body?" he said with more than a little laughter in his tone.

"No. Yes. No. Shit, after it was done, all I wanted was to know your name, but I didn't think of that until I was on the damn plane, and then I convinced myself if I did know your name, it would make it all real. And I would just fuck it all up anyway." There was obviously more that Mitch wanted to say, but he cut himself off. It sounded like Mitch wished he'd stayed and maybe had had a talk with Isaac, figured out a way to explore what was between them. But that couldn't be it.

So that was the issue? Mitch was angry at himself? "You're not making any sense. I think you're just pissed at yourself for fucking up with the son of the man who's paying for all this." Isaac held up his hands as he indicated their exotic surroundings. "You're worried about your job, your reputation, your—"

He didn't get any further as Mitch hauled him in and kissed him hard and fast. Isaac didn't argue; he couldn't if he tried. Mitch was strength and force, and all Isaac wanted was to lose himself in the kiss. He wanted what he'd never had with anyone else. He wanted what he'd had at Christmas. Honesty.

He attempted to pull back, and Mitch let him move only far enough to talk.

"Mitch."

"I want you again," Mitch said. He was breathing heavily, and his face had that familiar determination etched into every line.

"I'm not an escort," Isaac insisted as he attempted to wriggle free. He wasn't doing this. It didn't matter that the memories and the taste of this man was enough to have him hard and needy. If Mitchell wanted casual sex, then he and Isaac were not on the same page.

Mitch shook his head. "I know that. I don't want… Look, do you think that I can just switch off what I'm feeling right now?" He moved that single step closer and placed his hands on Isaac's waist. "Can we just start something for this week? Flirt a little? Have drinks? Then maybe when this is all over, we could go on a date and hope I don't fuck things up before they really begin?"

Isaac blinked at the man, lost in his eyes. He wanted something a bit sooner than waiting until they got back on the mainland. He was so turned on by the desire that sparked inside Mitch.

He took matters into his own hands and pressed his hard cock against Mitch's thigh. They were similar in height, Mitch maybe a couple inches taller, but pressed together Isaac could feel the evidence that Mitch was just as turned on as he was. Hell, just on memories of Christmas alone, Isaac was close to jumping Mitch's bones and being done with it.

"Whatever happened, however the hell we got here, I think the two of us on a beautiful island needs to be something we explore." Mitch moved him, pressing him back against the solid weight of a wooden panel behind him. Isaac was so turned on he could come right now. Mitch used both hands to grip Isaac's ass, and they kissed quickly before separating.

"I want to do this right," Mitchell said. "But first I just wanted to say —"

"Don't," Isaac snapped.

Mitch cupped his chin and tilted his face up. "Isaac?"

Isaac knew what he was going to say, and he didn't want to hear it. "Don't say you're sorry about Christmas again."

"I wasn't going to say sorry."

Isaac waited for more, but Mitch seemed more intent on staring at him than talking. "What were you going to say, then?"

"Thank you, that's all. For giving this thing a chance."

* * * * *

Isaac was in a daze as they walked back to the pool. Things weren't what he'd expected after seeing the same man he'd torn up the bed sheets with here on the island.

They didn't touch as they walked and neither spoke. As if by agreement, they separated when they got to the pool. Isaac didn't know where Mitch went, but Mitch's pants were wet from the pool water on Isaac, so Isaac imagined his room was the destination. Instead, Isaac just focused on crossing to Bruno and sitting on the longer.

As soon as he sat down he reran everything that had happened. None of it seemed real. What would happen next? In fact, what the hell had just happened? Why was Mitch so thankful about a chance? Isaac wasn't agreeing to a future date just to be nice, although it sounded to him that Mitch might think that was the case. Confusion mixed with the excitement of what he'd agreed to. A date, talking, beers, maybe some more of that kissing.

"You okay?" Bruno asked as he turned onto his front. The photographer was turning a nice shade of pink, which Isaac assumed would brown, otherwise why would he be sitting in the sun?

"Yeah," he said. He didn't feel capable of saying any more.

"That Mitch guy seems kind of stern," Bruno said.

"Nah," Isaac offered. He lay down and stared up at the blue sky, thankful the movement of the sun meant he was now entirely in shade. The enormity of what had happened hit him again. "He's okay."

Bruno grunted, but Isaac had no idea what that meant. Instead he covered his face with his arms and enjoyed the best rest he'd had… since Christmas Day.

Chapter 7

A few fruity cocktails and having to sit through some of the most horrendous karaoke he had ever witnessed — it was a good thing these models had their looks — and Mitch had been glad to retire to his room for some peace at the end of the evening. Things had been better between him and Isaac, less awkward, and hell, they'd even engaged in idle conversation at the bar. However, waking to another beautiful day on the island, Mitch was suddenly struck with the realization of what it meant to have Isaac in such close quarters for the next week.

Granted, both of them had expressed interest in one another, but was it really such a great idea? Business and pleasure, did that ever end well? He sucked on his teeth as he stared in the mirror in his room. He'd toned down the professional look for the day, opting for smart khaki shorts and a lightweight green shirt. He looked at his open collar. He hadn't thought he'd miss wearing a tie quite as much as he did right now. It had always been something of a security blanket, being perfectly turned out was something to hide behind, and here he was now open and feeling a little vulnerable, contemplating letting someone in, someone he barely knew — and the only someone to ever get this under his skin since Dylan.

There was a knock on the door. "You ready?" Bruno called from the other side of the door.

Mitch checked himself again, then opened the door.

The photographer was dressed in what Mitch had declared Bruno-style after the fourth cocktail he'd tried, some champagne and fruit fizz — baggy khaki shorts and a red and black checked shirt over a black A-shirt. His hair was freshly washed, stuck up at various angles, and Mitch wondered if it felt as soft and fluffy as it looked. Bruno sure had the grunge-puppy look down pat.

"All set?" Bruno asked again.

They were taking Isaac on a tour of the island to finalize the agreed segments for the shoots. Tomorrow was to be the first, keeping it sexy and modern with the obligatory pool shoot.

"Yeah," Mitch said, though he regretted the obvious lack of interest in his tone. He had the sneaking suspicion Bruno thought he was a bit of a dick and some hardass who rarely cracked a smile. He tried again. "Yes. Isaac's meeting us downstairs."

Bruno raised an eyebrow, but dismissed Mitch's enthusiastic one-eighty. "Are we starting anywhere in particular?"

Mitch pulled the door to his room closed as he stepped into the corridor. "I don't think he cared, was just interested in getting the lay of the land."

"Okay," Bruno said. He fell in step with Mitch as they headed for the stairs. He was clearly considering the various locations he'd scouted the previous days.

"I suggest ending somewhere with some punch. Maybe the spring?" Mitch found a big finish was usually the way to go, and the spring was certainly a grand backdrop with the pool and small waterfall.

Bruno nodded. "Cool, if we start here and head down to the beach, we can work our way up to the spring and back down on the opposite beach. That will bring us around in a nice loop."

Isaac was waiting for them when they got downstairs. "Good morning," he said cheerily.

Having taken his breakfast in his room, Mitch hadn't really seen anyone that morning and had yet to slip into sociable conversation mode. He gave Isaac a nod by way of a greeting and checked out the man's rather short denim shorts. Combined with a loose-fitting white shirt open to just above his navel showing off his defined abs, and it was obvious Isaac had taken to the tropical surroundings. Mitch eyed Isaac's thighs below the hem of the shorts. The thought of getting Isaac out of them had him smirking to himself, but he quickly realized Isaac had noticed when he tugged on the bottom of his shirt.

Bruno narrowed his eyes and looked between the two men. He looked like he had questions, but Mitch wasn't about to indulge him.

"Shall we get started?" Mitch said. He slapped Bruno on the back. "Do you want to lead the way?"

"Sure," Bruno said. He turned his attention to Isaac, enthusing about his exploration of the island before Isaac's arrival.

Mitch put on his shades and let Bruno take the lead. They started by the pool, discussing how they might make what he called 'traditional' shots edgier and fit with the grittier survivalist feel Isaac wanted while also weaving the agreed-upon theme of red into the pictures. Mitch stood and listened. He was damn impressed by what Bruno was saying, and it became apparent why Isaac had pressed to get the photographer for the Bailey's brand.

"There are lights in the pool plus we can get some more on the pool edge. I suggest red and blue filters in there when we get the models in the water. Light the models up, especially the girls and the larger, lightweight dresses and the like. Half-submerged, material spread out, dark makeup. Kind of a mermaid, siren, lady-in-the-lake type of thing going on." Bruno spoke with his hands.

Isaac nodded. He was seemingly mesmerized by Bruno's words.

"Obviously, we'll mix it up with some normal shots. Plus, I thought on the pool edge we'd maybe thread red through the background depending on the outfits. Don't want some garish clash going on." Bruno laughed. "But we have streamers for among the plants, some pots we can sit plants in. The boys who work here said they'd help heft those around. Plus we have some red—" He waved his fingers toward his hair as he searched for the correct description. "—clip-in hair extension things for the girls and other stuff." Excitement was etched on his face, but he stopped, suddenly embarrassed. "But you probably know all that from the outline I gave you."

"Seeing it on paper and listening to you are two totally different things," Isaac assured him.

Bruno smiled. "Shall we move on?"

"Let's," Isaac said.

The rest of the tour followed a similar pattern. Bruno would enthusiastically describe in detail what he'd planned, from the red glow of a campfire on the beach to the spray of the small falls at the spring, and Isaac wore an excited expression. At one point Mitch thought Isaac might burst into song and skip along the sand, the man looked so in awe of everything Bruno was saying for the shoot.

Finding a spot in the shade of a palm, Mitch crouched and picked idly at the tuft of beach grass at his feet. He picked a blade and ran his fingers over the slightly rough length.

"Sorry if this is boring you," Bruno said as he joined him in the shade.

Mitch tossed the grass to one side. "No, it's been great to hear your plans." He looked up at Bruno before the man sat on the ground next to him.

"You're bored as hell, right?" Bruno grinned.

"Maybe. Just a bit." He laughed. "It's nice to see him so interested, though."

"Isaac?" Bruno pursed his lips as he looked to where Isaac was investigating the edge of the spring pool.

Mitch nodded. "He's really impressed by you. He seems happy with everything."

"And that's important to you?"

Mitch caught the glint of interest in Bruno's eyes. "Of course," Mitch said. "He's my client." He leaned toward Bruno. "Plus his daddy's paying the bills."

From behind his shades, he watched Isaac, who had made himself comfortable on the rocks around the pool, removed his shoes, and put his feet in the water. The look of absolute peace on Isaac's face as he closed his eyes and tilted his head up toward the sun was gorgeous. Awkwardly, Mitch shifted his attention, brushing a hand through his hair as he looked at the ground. Isaac really wasn't playing fair looking so damn hot. First the shorts, now the perfect pose in the perfect setting. Was he purposely trying to break the professional exterior Mitch was attempting to maintain?

With a grunt, Mitch sat down properly and rested against the tree.

"I'm going to head back to the hotel," Bruno said loudly. "I need to call my girlfriend and email a couple of people about gigs next month."

Mitch did his best not to tut. He'd just gotten comfortable.

"Okay." Isaac pulled his feet out of the water.

"Oh, no. You guys stay," Bruno insisted. "Make the most of the quiet."

Before either Isaac or Mitch could protest, Bruno was back on his feet and had jogged off between the trees. Neither of them said anything at first, but eventually the silence was too much for Mitch.

"How's the water?" he asked. God, that was lame.

Isaac leaned back. He briefly looked at Mitch, then turned back to the water. "Why don't you come over here and find out for yourself?"

Mitch eyed the gap. *Because there'd be nothing stopping me from grabbing you and kissing you.*

"Bruno is very good," Isaac said when it was clear Mitch wasn't going to be lured over so easily. "He just gets it."

Mitch touched the corner of his shades, dropping them down his nose. "Guy certainly has a vision."

Isaac nodded slowly as he smiled. With a sigh, he got to his feet and came to Mitch. "Were you just going to leave me sitting there?"

What was he supposed to say? He waited as Isaac sat down beside him and leaned back against the tree. "I didn't want to assume," he said.

"That's very sweet of you." Isaac sat forward. "But a little assumption wouldn't hurt."

Chuckling, Mitch leaned his head back. "You're sure about this?"

"I meant what I said. I don't care how we got here. I just don't think we should throw away a night that you have to admit was pretty fun."

There was no way Mitch could argue with that. Christmas Eve had been amazing. Not wanting to say something stupid, Mitch leaned forward, kissing Isaac. Pulling back, he blinked and looked into Isaac's eyes. In the light, Isaac's eyes were the color of a delicious caramel, and the man himself was just as yummy.

He looked away for a moment, playing in his head the outcomes of what they were doing. All he could think about were the words he'd heard more than once from more than one person. *Life's too short. Money isn't everything.* Maybe not everything was about money and sealing the deal. Those didn't matter right now, anyway. The job here on Sapphire Cay was already a done thing, contracts signed, payments made.

Isaac waited. Mitch knew he wanted more than just his signature and a handshake.

Christ, Mitch was so used to having his head in the game, always prepared for anything. He was confused, but from the way his chest tightened just having Isaac close to him, he knew that as unexpected as it was, he kind of liked it. He'd already admitted to Isaac that Isaac was in his head, and as much as he wanted to ignore it, he didn't think the feeling would go away anytime soon. Not while they were stuck on an island together with nowhere to run.

It was probably the wrong thing to say, but he had to make sure Isaac was clear on one thing. Whatever his thoughts about life and money, he had to think about his career if he was really honest. "Business should come first."

Isaac didn't say anything. He leaned forward and tilted his head slightly as he looked over Mitch's face. "I don't plan on letting anything or anyone distract me from this shoot."

From the look on Isaac's face, Mitch could tell Isaac was serious. Mitch knew how important the launch of the brand was to Bailey's.

"But we're not working now, right?" Isaac moved in, laying small teasing kisses on Mitch's lips.

"No." Mitch smiled. "No, we're not." He wrapped his hand in the front of Isaac's shirt and pulled him into an open-mouthed kiss. The kiss was slow but heated. Mitch held Isaac's face, caressing his jaw, and he couldn't help but smile as they kissed.

The intensity between them grew, and kisses turned to silent exploration of each other's body. Mitch breathed in deeply, holding Isaac close as he felt the other man's touch. Isaac ran his hands down over Mitch's stomach, teasingly across the bulge in his pants, and rested on his thigh. Isaac's hands were hot through the material of Mitch's shorts, and Mitch struggled to suppress the urge to buck up into the man's palm. He wanted friction and ultimately a release from the feelings building inside him.

The sound of Isaac's phone broke them out of the moment, and Isaac pulled back. He planted what felt like a final kiss on Mitch's mouth and wriggled free from Mitch's hold.

"Leave it," Mitch said. They couldn't stop now. He wanted more. He wanted Isaac here and to himself in this beautiful secluded part of the island.

Isaac licked his lips and gently wiped his mouth. "Just…" He slid his phone out of his pocket and eyed the screen. "It's a text message from my dad." He rocked back on his heels and pushed himself to his feet. "He wants me to call him and check in. I should get this."

Mitch looked at Isaac. "Seriously?"

Isaac shrugged and pocketed his phone. He checked his surroundings, and Mitch assumed he was mentally plotting a route back to the hotel.

"Hey." Mitch reached for his hand, gently brushing Isaac's fingers with his own.

Briefly, Isaac leaned down, catching Mitch's mouth in a kiss. Standing up, he smiled as he used Mitch's words against him, saying before walking away, "Business first."

Chapter 8

Mitch sat on the end of the bed and rested his head in his hands. Gently he moved his fingers in soothing circles against his temples and closed his eyes. He'd skipped lunch, and apart from a couple of hours when he had been practically dragged out of his room by Bruno to socialize over a second night of cocktails and a buffet supper, Mitch had stayed upstairs. He wouldn't say he'd been avoiding Isaac, or anyone else for that matter, but after the failed rendezvous at the spring, he just needed some downtime and a moment to stop and step back. Losing himself in emails and contracts was better than any cold shower right now. Doris had finally sent the information through about the Weston contract and the potential deal, a worthy focus for his energy. And he tried to concentrate, he really did, but his thoughts kept returning to earlier.

Business should come first. Christ, had he really said that? As much as he'd like to think that he'd spent the last few hours being productive, the reality was the complete opposite. He'd sat in front of his laptop, but all he could think about was Isaac.

Mitch knew he'd been an idiot and had the niggling feeling of déjà vu. He'd screwed everything up with Dylan, gotten his priorities messed up and now he was doing it all again with Isaac. Yes, the contract and the shoot were important, and maybe mixing business and pleasure might be an unforgivable move if things went sour between them. But when Mitch thought about Isaac, all he could think was "fuck it." Isaac was worth the risk, worth putting first.

Though seeing him again had been a shock, it was also an incredible coincidence. Isaac was a true professional as he worked. The buzz of having Isaac here on the island, the thought of him standing in front of him dressed in nothing but swimwear, his hair damp and mussed... Mitch blinked. Fuck, that image alone might be worth every future contract he might ever make. Somehow, the fantasy that had stuck with Mitch since that night in the hotel in Miami had held up to the very real and very solid man he'd reconnected with.

Mitch remembered back to Christmas Eve. They really had fucked over the bathtub. Fucked in every square inch of that suite. He shifted as he realized what his imagination was doing to him and looked down at the bulge beneath the material of his pants. Blowing out a breath, he sat up and rubbed a hand over his bare chest. He massaged his collarbone as he looked up at the overhead fan. He'd thought he was used to the heat in Miami, but this was something else. He missed his temperamental A/C unit and his massive refrigerator with its built-in ice machine. Actually, ice sounded good.

Grabbing the ice bucket from the dresser by the door, he headed out into the corridor. The hotel had quite a few rooms across the second and third floors, with the kitchen, dining rooms, and Dylan and Lucas's office and living space situated on the ground floor. Taking a right out of his room, Mitch made his way along the hallway and through the door into the stairs. It was cooler in the stairwell than his room. Also on his floor were Isaac, Bruno, and four of the models.

Mitch stopped on the landing and looked out the window, which overlooked the back of the hotel. Night had crept in, but he could make out a few people still on the patio beneath the low lighting around the pool. He stood on tiptoe and leaned forward against the glass. He wondered where Isaac was. Had he been accosted once again by the female model who had clearly taken a shine to him? Mitch suppressed the twinge of jealousy at the memory of her hanging off Isaac's arm at supper. She wasn't Isaac's type. He was damn sure of that. With a smirk, he continued his descent and exited the stairs into the entrance hall. There was no one around. With the only light from a handful of lamps, the hotel seemed even eerier than earlier.

Where to get ice? He hadn't passed any machines. He looked at the patio doors, making out the empty bar. Scott had already stopped serving drinks. He eyed the door to the kitchen and the 'staff only' sign. Well, he knew staff—that totally counted, right? Hesitating, he looked around. He just wanted some ice. What was the worst that could happen?

The kitchen door swung shut behind him, and he stopped by the entrance. The kitchen was in darkness. Stepping forward, he ran his hand over the wall, successfully finding a light switch. He blinked as the fluorescent lights flickered to life, accompanied by the low buzz of power. Hugging the cool ice bucket to his chest, he walked the length of the kitchen. His first instinct was to check behind some of the cupboard doors for a concealed smaller freezer, but unsuccessful, he turned to the large walk-in units. The first was filled with fresh produce and funny-looking vegetables, or maybe they were fruits, that he'd never even seen before. Some were far too comical in shape to actually be real, surely?

The second unit was what he wanted, and he shuddered as he opened the door of the large freezer. Mitch rubbed at his arm as goose pimples raised across his skin. He examined the shelves, rejoicing when he found large bags of ice piled at the back of the freezer. He looked at the freezer door and pulled his hand away, concerned as the door moved, swinging shut.

What's the worst that could happen? he asked himself again. Apart from getting trapped in a freezer and freezing to death? Nothing much.

"What are you doing?"

"Jesus!" Mitch clutched his chest with one hand and juggled the ice bucket in the other. He took a moment before making eye contact with his light-footed companion. "You nearly gave me a heart attack."

Adam eyed him curiously and looked at the open freezer. "What are you doing?" he asked again.

"Ice," Mitch managed. He cleared his throat. "I'm fine, by the way."

Adam grinned and took the ice bucket from him. Pushing the door open wide, he crouched down and fastened the door open with a hook at its base. "Why didn't you call down to the desk?" he asked, proceeding to collect the ice.

"I wanted the walk. Besides, there was nobody there."

"Pee break," Adam informed him.

"Ah," Mitch said. Not knowing what to do with himself, he folded his arms across his chest and watched Adam shovel ice from an open bag.

Finished, Adam returned the full ice bucket and closed the freezer. "Anything else I can get you?"

"No. This is great." He held the chilled bucket. Some ice in a towel and he'd be in heaven. He edged back, waiting for Adam to join him before they left the kitchen. "Thanks."

"No worries and goodnight."

"Night," Mitch said and started back upstairs. Walking the corridor to his room, he was surprised when a door opened ahead of him and Isaac stuck out his head.

"Hey," Isaac said. "Are they keeping you awake too?"

"Who?"

Isaac ignored the question and his eyes widened as he looked excitedly at the bucket in Mitch's hands. "Is that ice?" He grabbed Mitch by the arm and dragged him into his room.

Stumbling forward, Mitch found himself standing in the middle of Isaac's room. He waited for Isaac to shut the door and join him. Mitch noted the sound of laughter outside. Isaac's room was on the pool side of the hotel, and he guessed the models and crew were enjoying the exotic setting—and possibly each other. He glanced over his shoulder. Not that he could blame them. He kept his eyes on Isaac, watching him from across the room as he headed to his dresser. When Isaac turned around, he was holding two tumblers and a bottle of whiskey.

"I may have stolen it. Or rather, Adam let me steal it. Stay for a drink?" Isaac held the glasses out to Mitch. "I'd appreciate the company."

Mitch took one of the tumblers and settled his gaze on Isaac's. There was a soft haze in Isaac's eyes, no doubt from the champagne at dinner followed by more alcohol on the patio. Pursing his lips, Mitch said, "Sure. Why not?"

* * * * *

"Dylan's your ex?" Isaac laughed. "Wow. I don't see it."

"What?" Mitch asked, cradling his glass in his hands as he lay on his side on the bed, propped up on his elbow. He wasn't entirely sure how agreeing to stay for a drink and looking through some of

Isaac's designs in his portfolio had turned to discussing Dylan and exes in general.

"The two of you. I mean he's so… and you're… not." Isaac sipped his drink, then shifted slightly. He was lying beside Mitch, mirroring Mitch's pose as he rested on one arm, his legs hanging over the end of the bed. "No offense," he added.

Mitch snorted a laugh. "It was a long time ago. When he had regular access to a hairdresser and owned a suit." Dylan had changed a lot since they had dated briefly. He always had been a free spirit locked inside a businessman, and it was kind of nice to see him finally be free, to soar.

Isaac smiled. "It must be weird seeing him again."

Shrugging, Mitch said, "It's not as weird as I thought it would be. We've both grown up a lot since then. He's happy and I'm…" Happy, too? Was he happy? "And I'm okay."

With a nod, Isaac asked, "So there's no one else, no one special back in Miami?"

Mitch swallowed more of the bitter whiskey and licked his lips. He met Isaac's eyes. Was Isaac fishing? "Since Dylan, the only long-term relationship I've had is with my cleaner." He looked away and slid his glass onto the nightstand. "Her name is Esther, and she collects pig ornaments."

"Pigs? Really? My mom collects frogs. They're everywhere. In the house, in the garden, every room. Go to the bathroom, and they're there, staring at you with their beady little frog eyes." He sighed and rested his head in his hand. He looked tired, drunk.

"Give me that," Mitch said and took Isaac's glass from him. He placed it on the table beside his. When he turned back, he was surprised to find Isaac had moved closer, crowding his space as he teased his gaze over Mitch's face until he settled his attention on Mitch's mouth.

"Did you know that I…" Isaac paused and rested his hand on Mitch's arm. "I have a degree in business?"

Mitch couldn't help but smile. Isaac wasn't what he'd expected. Being told the ex-model son of the company boss was overseeing things hadn't exactly been the news Mitch wanted to hear when Jerry had told him. Yes, Mitch was good at his job. He was good with order, the definite parts of life, the small print. He wasn't artistic, didn't know anything about colors or framing a shot, and his creative flair only went as far as working a contract in his favor. Jerry had laid the groundwork, but Mitch for once had felt like he wasn't going to be able to fill the cavernous boots Jerry had left for him.

"I didn't know that."

"Uh-huh. Not just a pretty face." Isaac leaned forward and rested his hand on Mitch's chest. He looked at Mitch through lust-heavy lids. Slowly, Isaac edged in until he was close enough to kiss Mitch. Firmly, he pressed his mouth to Mitch's and let out a soft sigh.

"Mmm." Pushing himself higher, Mitch threaded his fingers in the back of Isaac's hair, pulling the man close as they kissed. Kissing was good but... Their business-first mantra screamed in his head. Isaac was drunk—ish—and he had a big day ahead of him. "I should let you get some sleep," Mitch said.

Isaac looked disappointed. "You didn't seem to care about sleep the last time we found ourselves in a hotel room together."

Mitch massaged the back of Isaac's head, grinning when it seemed the other man might actually start to purr. "You weren't wasted then." Mitch had been tipsy, happy, but both of them had been very aware of what they were doing.

Isaac screwed up his mouth. "Fair point." He looked at Mitch and leaned in for another kiss. He nipped Mitch's lip before asking, "What's our call time for the first shoot?"

Idly, Mitch stroked the back of Isaac's hair. "Bruno's starting with the standard shots around the pool at eleven." He ran the back of his hand over Isaac's jaw. Isaac's skin was smooth, and Mitch admired his youthful looks. "Probably a good call considering the amount of alcohol some of them put away tonight." He ran his hand down over Isaac's shoulder, waist, and settled on Isaac's thigh. He fingered the hem of Isaac's cutoffs before slipping his hand beneath the material. Isaac's skin was clammy from the heat, and memories flooded Mitch's mind. He remembered Isaac's legs, slim yet strong as Isaac had wrapped them around his waist as they'd fucked for the second time Christmas Eve night. Christ, now he was horny and wanted nothing more than to give into temptation. Should he? Or should they wait before blurring forever the line between professional and personal desires?

"I know what I'm doing." Isaac breathed deeply, closing his eyes as he lifted his hip, guiding Mitch's touch higher. "I'm not a kid. I can handle my drink." He bobbed his head, teasing Mitch with pecked kisses as he looked for a response.

Desire flooded Mitch, rational thinking leaving him as he kissed Isaac soundly.

"You're no kid," Mitch growled and grabbed Isaac by his wrists. He rolled Isaac onto his back and straddled his thighs, swallowing heavily as Isaac rutted beneath him.

Pinning Isaac to the bed, he leaned over him and their mouths met in a sloppy, heated kiss. Mitch nipped and sucked, working a line of kisses from Isaac's mouth to nuzzle his neck and back again. His head spun as their bodies entwined, Isaac wriggling free of his hold to flip their positions and lie on top of Mitch between his legs. Heatedly, he ground against Mitch, causing friction. Mitch was so fucking hard. He wrapped his arms around Isaac, tightening his hold in Isaac's hair as he arched upward. Fuck, he was close. So fucking close. With a muted cry, he pressed his mouth greedily to Isaac's, stealing kisses as he rode out his orgasm.

Isaac grinned into the kiss and reached between them. He continued to kiss Mitch as he took hold of his erection, bringing himself off after a few rough tugs. With a grunt, he fell against Mitch, then rolled onto the bed beside him.

Mitch stared up at the ceiling fan as he caught his breath and listened to the heavy pants from Isaac as he did the same. Mitch closed his eyes, smiling when Isaac took his hand and intertwined their fingers. Neither man said anything, just enjoyed the shared quiet moment. The feeling of pure bliss mixed with alcohol and exhaustion eventually overwhelmed them both, but when he woke the next morning, Mitch would still remember the feel and warmth of Isaac curled up against him and hugging his waist.

* * * * *

Blinking, Mitch opened his eyes. Someone was knocking on the door, and Mitch was filled with the sudden panic that he was late. He was never late.

Isaac groaned and lifted his head from the pillow beside him. "What the hell?" he grumbled and slowly sat up.

Whoever was outside knocked again.

"All right!" Isaac called, causing them both to wince.

"What time is it?" Mitch asked.

Isaac took his watch from the nightstand. "Nine." With an annoyed grunt, he got off the bed and wandered toward the door.

Mitch licked his lips and grimaced at the taste of stale alcohol.

Isaac opened the door to a flustered-looking Bruno. "Bruno." Isaac leaned against the doorjamb as he rubbed tiredly at his face.

Bruno went to speak, only to stop when he spotted Mitch. "Oh, crap. Sorry." He hovered awkwardly, watching as Mitch got to his feet and joined Isaac at the door. "Shall I come back?"

Mitch considered making up an excuse, something ridiculous like he'd popped by early — without showering and with no shirt — to get Isaac to sign some papers that had inexplicably vanished. But there was no way that would sail, so he just smiled. "You're here now. What's up?"

Bruno looked serious as he said, "It's Yan."

Yan? Must be one of the models.

"What about him?"

Bruno shook his head like he couldn't believe what he was saying. "We've got a problem."

Chapter 9

Isaac stared at Yan in disbelief.

"What the fuck?" he said again. That was his fourth 'what the fuck,' but he could go for more if needed.

"I don't know," Yan said. Well, it sounded like that was what he said. He sounded miserable and his eyes were bloodshot.

"Holy shit," Lucas cursed from the door. "What happened?"

Dylan came to a halt behind him. "Shit."

"Do you have any antihistamine?" Mitch asked. Isaac glanced at him. Did Mitch have an idea of what the hell was going on?

"Yeah, I'll get the medical bag." Dylan left the main sitting area as quickly as he'd arrived.

Mitch guided poor Yan to sit on one of the sofas. "I think he's had an allergic reaction to something."

"I'll get Adam, he's had training," Lucas announced, then left in the same direction as Dylan.

Dylan returned first, and in his arms he held a huge medical box. With deft movements, he snapped open the lid and lifted it. The contents of the box were a medic's dream—an assortment of meds and even a portable defibrillator. Isaac guessed it wasn't easy to call for paramedics if they were needed on this far-flung speck of sand and soil in the middle of nowhere.

"Should we call for an airlift?" Mitch asked.

"Let's try an antihistamine first."

Yan moaned before slumping back on the sofa. Dylan was immediately all over the situation. He encouraged Yan to take meds and then carried out checks that Isaac found familiar and reassuring. The pulse, the pupils, checking airways.

Adam skidded into the room with Lucas and was at Yan's side in seconds. Seemed he and Dylan were a double team for the medical stuff. Within a few minutes, Yan was resting easily on the sofa and some of the swelling had gone down from his foot and leg. Dylan checked Yan's pulse and scribbled details onto a small sheet.

"Should we get him back to the mainland?" Lucas asked. Isaac thanked Lucas silently for asking the question Isaac was too freaked-out to ask. Poor Yan's leg looked like some reject from a zombie film, all puffy and scarlet, with a rash that was far from pretty.

"He was just swimming," Crystal said from behind Isaac. "We both were."

Isaac couldn't help it; he had been so focused on Yan that he jumped at the intrusion. She looked pointedly at him with a shake of her pretty head. Evidently he wasn't on her hit list anymore.

"Where?" Dylan asked immediately.

"Just off the jetty. We hadn't gone far, and then suddenly he just hopped about, cursing. He said something had stung him, but we couldn't see anything."

Adam immediately moved to Yan's feet and examined them closely. "Someone point a light," he ordered. Mitch reacted quickly and soon had a spotlight on poor Yan's swollen foot.

"There's a lot of edema," Adam said.

Isaac winced. That didn't sound like a good thing.

Dylan joined Adam at the feet of the now-softly snoring Yan, and the two men peered closely.

"Is that something?" Dylan asked and pointed at a part of the swollen foot. Adam scrutinized the spot before sitting back on his heels with a nod.

"Shit," he said. Then he stood from his crouch.

That sounded bad. "Do we need to get him to the mainland?" Isaac repeated his question. The whole situation appeared to be serious and he didn't want one of his models—hell, anyone really—dying in this place.

Adam shook his head. "Nematocyst," he said. "You agree, Dylan?" Dylan nodded. "I'll get the vinegar." And with that, he left.

"What's a nematocyst?" Isaac asked.

"A poisonous barb," Dylan offered. "He probably stood on something without realizing it. For some people it's an itching irritant, for others like our guy here, there could be a more obvious reaction. Sleep and some antihistamines and he'll be fine. We just need to get the barb out of his foot."

Isaac grimaced. "Can we do anything to help?"

"How long will he be ill?" Mitch asked

Isaac and Mitch spoke at the same time, Isaac not at all worried about timescales and Mitch clearly in business mode.

Adam returned with vinegar, and Isaac watched as Dylan used it to wipe at Yan's foot before using tweezers and antiseptic wipe. He was concentrating hard and neither Isaac or Mitch interrupted what looked like a delicate procedure.

"Couple days, maybe a bit more," Adam offered. "Rashes like this could last up to three days. I'll keep an eye on him. We'll get him back to his room, but mostly he just needs to sleep this off."

Isaac got the sense they were being dismissed, and he gripped Mitch and Crystal by the arms and proceeded to usher them out. Crystal balked at the action and instead twisted free.

"I'll stay and get him settled," she said pleasantly enough but with a thread of steel in her voice. Isaac would have laughed if it hadn't been such a serious situation.

"First shoot is at eleven," Mitch reminded Crystal. The words caused Isaac to look at his watch. Half past nine. Had only thirty minutes passed since Bruno knocked on their door? It felt like hours.

Speaking of Bruno, he'd disappeared after turning gray and looking like he was going to faint. Isaac really needed to check in on the photographer.

"I'll be there," Crystal said with a toss of her brown hair.

Mitch walked down the shaded corridor and out into the foyer of the hotel. Scott manned the desk, sitting back in his tilted chair with his long legs crossed in front of him.

"Everything okay?" Scott asked with a welcoming smile like nothing at all was wrong.

"You don't seem worried about Yan," Isaac snapped.

Scott sat up in his chair. "Why? Is it serious?" he asked with genuine confusion.

"He's all swollen and rashy and now he's snoring."

Scott blinked up at Isaac. "Snoring?" He smiled and relaxed. "Ahh, he got stung, didn't he?" The words were not a question, more a statement. "And Adam and Dylan have it under control."

"Still, I would have thought—"

Mitch stopped him with a touch to his arm. "Everything is fine," he said softly.

Isaac stepped back and away from him. He'd chosen this exotic location, and he'd been the one to select somewhere that could put a man's life at risk. How was that okay?

Mitch looked at him directly and raised one of his eyebrows in a silent question, probably something about what was going on in Isaac's head, and how Yan was fine, and how it was all done now, and how Isaac should just calm the fuck down. All that with just one eyebrow and the teasing in his gorgeous sapphire eyes.

"Sorry," Isaac said to Scott without taking his eyes off Mitch. Then he turned on his heel to leave and ran straight into Bruno.

"Everything okay?" Bruno asked. He was weighed down with cameras, and his bright red hair had been pulled back from his face into a short ponytail. "Yan looked like shit."

"Allergic reaction," Mitch answered for Isaac. Isaac was grateful. He needed air and was out the main door and onto the sand by the jetty before he consciously thought about what he was doing. He leaned over and rested his hands on his knees, attempting to settle his breathing.

"Isaac?" Mitch asked. "You okay?"

No. This is messed up. I'm messing this up. "Dad had said we should cancel this, said it would get fucked up somehow."

Mitch rubbed Isaac's back in slow circles. "Nothing is fucked up. Yan will be okay, no damage done."

"Apart from the fact I'm down by a model for up to three days."

"So we'll reschedule the shoots —"

Panic swelled inside Isaac. "We can't do that." He'd thought he had a handle on the photo shoot and the island and, hell, his future. Then suddenly there was a slip in control.

"We'll get another model—"

Isaac straightened. "We can't do that either. We're on an island in the middle of freaking nowhere."

Mitch sighed heavily, then yanked Isaac close and kissed him. Not just a small touch of reassurance, but a bent-over-backward no-holds-barred iron-dick-in-his-pants kind of kiss. Isaac struggled a little at first as the panic he was experiencing was too much for even one of Mitch's kisses to overcome, but then suddenly, the panic fled. Abruptly he was limp in Mitch's hold and enjoying every second of the kiss. Maybe Mitch was a mind reader, maybe he just realized Isaac was calming down, but as quickly as he'd grabbed Isaac, he released him. The only thing that kept Isaac standing was the fact that Mitch steadied him before letting out a chuckle.

Isaac frowned. "Aren't you supposed to slap someone who's in mid-meltdown?" he asked and pressed his fingers to his bruised, well-kissed lips. "Not kiss them?"

Mitch leaned in for one more kiss before pulling back. "I prefer the kissing technique," he admitted.

"That's not reassuring. Are you going to go kissing anyone who gets panicky?"

Mitch smiled that infuriating smile of his. "Only the sexy ones named Isaac," he said. Mitch pushed his hands into the pockets of his dark shorts. This was not the first time over the last day that Isaac had wished he could get Mitch out of the shorts and loose shirt and into a pair of the low-slung board shorts that formed part of his designs.

Mitch was all cut and muscled with a soft dark blond furring of hair on his chest and a tantalizingly dark treasure trail that would disappear nicely into the band of the bright scarlet-and-black shorts. Perhaps as part of this makeover he was imagining, Isaac could persuade Mitch to stop slicking back his hair. Isaac worried his lower lip with his teeth as he attempted to pull himself out of fantasyland and figure out what to do next.

"We should replace Yan for some of the earlier shots," Isaac said finally. "I pulled him in specifically for his look, and he's a loss to this shoot, and fuck, I can't delay this without screwing this whole thing up."

"So, you need someone about five ten with dark hair that can be messy-styled, a slim but muscled body, and dark inscrutable eyes?"

Isaac nodded. He considered the guys on the island. Scott was too muscled, tanned, and too bulky, and Dylan wasn't too far behind him. Adam maybe? He didn't have a classic model look, gorgeous but no. And Lucas? Mitch imagined Lucas saying he was too old for modeling, despite being very pretty.

No, he needed something very definite. Then he realized Mitch had his arms crossed over his chest, his head tilted, and his stare directed at Isaac. "Sounds like you."

Surely Mitch wasn't thinking that Isaac could get in front of a camera again. "No way. No. Just. No."

"We could talk to Bruno about using you from angles that wouldn't drag you back to being a model. Or we could play up the designer angle?"

"I left that behind," Isaac said. He could be stubborn if he wanted to be, and being a model when he was sixteen was one thing, but now? He was twenty-six, a fashion designer. He was on the *other* side of the lens. Hell, he already got grief for being an ex-model. Even his dad underestimated him because he'd once posed for the camera. What hope was there for anyone in the fashion world taking him seriously as a designer if he gave in?

"Yeah, I know you did," Mitch said evenly.

"This is ridiculous."

Mitch shrugged. "You've got a body to die for." He said it so matter-of-factly, like that wasn't going to get Isaac's mouth to drop open in surprise.

"What?"

"You heard what I said. You have a body to die for, and I haven't been able to get you out of my head since Christmas." Mitch stepped forward and was suddenly right up in Isaac's space.

"Yeah?"

"Yeah. All long legs and toned, climbing me like a tree and wrapped around me all the way to heaven." Mitch uncrossed his arms and dug his hands deep into Isaac's hair. "And all this *gorgeous* hair really would look good on camera."

Isaac signed inwardly. Surely they had other options. They could wait three days. That still gave them a couple of days' clear shooting, with a couple more for fill-in work. They could give Yan the time he needed to look less like a zombie and more like the model he was. But everything would be so tight.

"Just when I was getting to build myself as a designer," Isaac said sadly. "No one took me seriously. Like an ex-model who looks twenty-one even though he's twenty-six doesn't have a brain and isn't worth anything. Then just this last year I was finally getting there. I know I'm not the best out there but—"

He was cut off as Mitch stole a kiss full of exasperation and heat. When Mitch pulled back, he had fire in his eyes, and damn if Isaac didn't feel weak at the knees.

"Shh," Mitch ordered. "You're worth everything. Now let's go talk to Bruno."

Chapter 10

"This is such a bad idea."

Isaac was more up and down than the boat ride from Marsh Harbor and was making Mitch feel equally nauseated.

"Will you just stop?" Mitch said on a laugh. He held Isaac by the shoulders but resisted the urge to shake some sense into the man. "Just stop, okay?"

Isaac took a deep breath and raised his hands, shaking out his anxiety. They'd delayed the shoot until the afternoon to give Isaac, Mitch, and Bruno time to tweak the arrangements for the next two days. Today was the pool, tomorrow the beach, then a day's break, by which time Yan would be back on his feet, before heading inland to the slice of heaven that was the spring including a shack, a waterfall, vegetation—the first of the grittier-looking backdrops and props in comparison to the pretty little things prancing around the side of a pool.

It was clear doubt still had a hold on Isaac. "It's been years. Do you know how many pizzas I've eaten since I last modeled?" He ran his hands over his stomach.

"If you even think about calling yourself fat, I may have to mess up your hair."

Isaac huffed a breath. "Don't you dare."

Mitch ran his hands up and down over the thin cotton shirt Isaac was wearing. "Do I need to kiss you again? You'll be fine. We've talked it through. You, me, Bruno, we're all on the same page. This will be great." He wished Isaac looked convinced. They'd decided they could use the designer angle, group shots around him, almost framing him among the other models and his designs.

"Promise?" Isaac lifted his head.

"I promise," Mitch said. The way Mitch figured it, Isaac should get involved with the shoot, hang-ups or not, and then once it got through to selecting photos for advertising and catalogues, Isaac could pull anything he didn't think promoted him, his brand, and his designs in the correct way.

There was a vulnerability about Isaac that Mitch hadn't seen before, and he was torn between keeping up the ever-professional business front he put on and just pulling Isaac close and hugging him.

"Now you go out there and give them your best Blue Steel," Mitch quipped.

Isaac sighed. "I might hate you a little bit."

Mitch laughed. Encouragingly, he squeezed Isaac's shoulders and very carefully, so as not to undo hair and makeup's hard but unnecessary work, leaned in and gently kissed Isaac. As far as he was concerned, Isaac didn't need any help to look good. The man was all-natural gorgeous, doe-eyed pretty. He released Isaac and stepped back to look his lover over. The shirt Isaac was wearing was lightweight and short-sleeved, one piece of the summer collection Bailey's was putting out in the coming months. It had a stylized logo of vines interlocked with a B on the shirt pocket to distinguish it. The shirt was tailored and fit Isaac's slim waist to perfection.

Clearing his throat, Isaac smoothed the front of the shirt. He wore the neck open, exposing his chest, and Mitch would have liked nothing more than to reach over and run his hands over Isaac's hot body once again.

"Okay?" Isaac checked. He teased the front of his hair and stood up straight. The rest of his outfit consisted of dark gray board shorts with a larger version of the B logo embellished with a black and white leaf and a wave design printed on one of the hips and down one leg, and set off with Isaac's own custom gray-and-green checked tennis shoes.

Mitch smiled. "Perfect," he said.

"We're all set out here," Bruno informed them as he leaned through the patio doors. "Ready?"

Isaac didn't speak but gave Bruno a sound nod. When Bruno left, he turned to Mitch. "Am I doing the right thing?"

Mitch saw Isaac stepping in as a nonissue. "Of course you are." He folded his arms across his chest and insisted confidently, "And once you're out there and involved, you'll see that too."

"Okay," he said, briefly glancing over his shoulder. "Let's get on with it."

* * * * *

"What do you call a group of models?" Dylan asked.

Mitch leaned back in his seat and eyed the group on the opposite side of the pool. "I don't know. What do you call a group of models?"

Dylan looked at him blankly. "It wasn't a joke. I was being serious."

"And toward me," Mitch heard Bruno call. The photographer dipped and weaved, taking various shots from different angles.

"Does Lucas know you're sitting out here with me ogling scantily clad swimwear models?" Mitch picked up his phone and checked the time. The shoot had broken the three-hour mark, and Mitch was finding it hard to keep smiling. With breaks for outfit changes, refreshments, and reapplying sun block as the models had shots in and around the pool and patio, the afternoon seemed to be dragging. As nice as it was to watch the half-dressed men and women posing in the sunshine or emerging from the pool with wet and clinging costumes, Mitch was itching to do something, anything.

"Sure. He'd be out here too if Edward hadn't phoned to talk wedding stuff." Dylan folded his arms across his chest and leaned back in his seat. "I don't know who's worse when it comes down to the perfect shade of purple for the napkins."

Putting down his cell, Mitch picked up the cold drink Dylan had brought out only moments ago. He eyed the glass, pretty sure his drink was more ice than anything else. Distracted by said swimwear models, Mitch sucked slowly on the straw and watched the models from over the top of his sunglasses.

Despite Isaac's initial misgivings, he had easily slipped back into the fold with the five original models. How hard could it be to turn and pout and pose? Actually, harder than Mitch realized. He was growing tired just sitting and watching even without having to actually listen, follow the photographer's instructions, and stand in the scorching sun at the correct angle trying to look like the definition of perfect.

Throughout the afternoon, the three female models had pouted and flaunted around in bikinis and floral dresses. They each held their own elements of beauty, some more appealing to Mitch than others. Their body types differed from stick-thin and nowhere near a handful to slim but curvy with thighs Mitch was sure could crush a guy to death, all toned, tanned, and smooth. The male models were equally beautiful. The younger of the two was too fair for Mitch's taste, with swept-back blond hair that sat in waves on the top of his head and curled behind his ears. He had an ethereal look about him, high cheekbones and elfin features. Maybe he'd just stepped out of Middle Earth, Mitch mused. The other model was darker in coloring, more rugged than Isaac, with short hair and catlike eyes.

Mitch watched Bruno as he arranged the models around Isaac. Isaac was seated on a stool. Barefoot and shirtless, Isaac sat with his back straight and turned slightly to the left as the other models crowded around him. Bruno directed the men to crouch down in front and to position themselves in such a way to show the patterned swimwear. The female models then stood around Isaac, one on either side and Crystal behind him. Crystal rested her hands on Isaac's shoulders, standing slightly to Isaac's right to enable a clear view of the rounded curves of her ample cleavage in the halter-neck swimsuit.

Dylan's laughing beside him pulled Mitch from his observation. He eyed his old love, who pursed his lips and quirked an eyebrow.

"What?" Mitch asked.

"She's persistent. I'll give her that." Dylan nodded toward the group.

Mitch looked back, noting the curl of Crystal's fingers against Isaac's shoulders, the way she slid her hands downward, and the way she pressed her nails against Isaac's chest. It seemed Yan was forgotten, at least for the moment.

"Nothing to do with me," he said and focused on his drink.

"Really?" Dylan sat forward and leaned on the back of Mitch's chair. "Your big goofy face tells me different."

Mitch silently played with his straw, stirring his drink.

"You talked."

Mitch looked over his shoulder. "I guess we did."

Dylan smiled. "And?" Dylan was an ex. This conversation shouldn't be happening, right? "Are you and he..." Dylan was clearly waiting for Mitch to jump in and finish for him.

"Honestly," Mitch started. He looked at Isaac. The group had moved away from serious and sexy to light and fun frolicking in the sun as Bruno continued to take shots. Isaac was smiling. Just watching the man had Mitch desperate to wrap his fingers in Isaac's mussed hair and drag him caveman-style back to his hotel room. He wasn't sure how, but Isaac was under his skin and dangerously close to stealing his heart. "I don't know." There, he'd said it. Though things were great here in their little bubble of paradise, could that really translate out there in the real world? Did they stand a chance when they returned to Miami?

"You can't hide behind your contracts and profit forever," Dylan stated. "If you think he could be the one…"

Mitch looked at Dylan, horrified. Was he that obvious? Yes, he liked Isaac. He liked spending time with him and the attraction was there. He turned around and was filled with a strange feeling as Isaac's eyes met his. God, the man was amazing, even more so when he smiled at Mitch. Fuck, if this had been a movie, Mitch would expect camera flare and a slow-motion zoom in on Isaac's face as he shyly lowered his head and closed his eyes. Sadly, it was real life, and when Isaac simply raised an eyebrow, Mitch realized he'd been staring. Still was.

Clearing his throat, Mitch forced himself to look away, only to regret it when he was once again face to face with Dylan.

"Like I said. I don't know." He pushed the straw to one side and took a drink of his lemonade, working the tiny remains of an ice cube into his mouth. Sitting back, he sucked on the ice as he thought about Isaac.

"Well, maybe it's time you figured it out," Dylan suggested. He'd found his perfect man, was getting married, and now what? Suddenly he was some kind of love guru?

Mitch scratched at the metal tabletop, picking at a small raised blemish beneath the painted surface. He crunched the ice, swallowing it before saying, "My life is just so..." He sighed. "It's high pressure, stressful, late nights, and I come home and *I* can't stand to be near me."

Dylan shook his head. "I'm not telling you that you need to be like me or Lucas or anyone else. It's just... Believe it or not, I still care about you. I'd like to think we're still friends, kind of, in some weird way." He grinned and rested his hand on Mitch's shoulder. "I just like to see everyone happy." He tilted his head and flashed a smile. "I'll leave you to it."

"What?" Confused, Mitch frowned as Dylan got to his feet, but then realized someone was standing behind him.

"Food is ready in an hour." Dylan directed his statement beyond Mitch before heading inside.

Mitch turned around as Isaac sat down beside him. Isaac looked happy, and clearly getting involved in front of the camera hadn't been the terrible experience he had feared. "Did you have fun?"

Isaac picked up Mitch's drink and took a sip. "Uh-huh." He leaned forward and planted a kiss on Mitch's cheek.

"What was that for?"

"For sitting here in the sun, bored out of your mind for what? Three hours? And supporting me."

Snorting a laugh, Mitch shrugged. "Not like I had anything better to do."

In one swift move, Isaac reached out and picked up Mitch's phone. He held it firmly in front of him. "I'm sure you had plenty you could have been doing."

Isaac was right. Mitch could have easily stolen away and sat with his laptop up in his room. But he hadn't wanted to. He'd wanted to be here for Isaac, to be the support and assurance Isaac had needed to get up there and do what he had to.

Mitch chewed on his lip and took the phone from Isaac's hand. "It's fine. It's my job."

"Just your job?" There was an expectant look in Isaac's eyes. Mitch recognized the mix of emotion and need.

"So Dylan said the food is an hour, right?" Mitch asked. He touched Isaac's thigh and teasingly ran his hand upward over heated skin.

Isaac flattened his hand over Mitch's, halting his progress before he edged beneath the material of Isaac's trunks. "I believe so."

"Then how about we head inside?"

"Another part of your job?" Isaac's words seemed sad if anything.

Mitch leaned in and shook his head. "That depends," he said.

"On what?"

Gently, Mitch stroked the back of his hand over Isaac's jaw. He leaned in and kissed Isaac soundly on the mouth. "What do you want?"

Isaac appeared to think about the question. In a low voice, he confessed, "I like you." He squeezed his hand around Mitch's. "I get that this place and this whole situation is intense and crazy, and we've kind of been thrown together, but what I feel started at Christmas and hasn't changed even after getting to know you. Here or back in Miami, I'd really like to explore it." He paused and lowered his head, clearly fearing he'd said too much.

Mitch had needed to hear that. He pressed his mouth to Isaac's shoulder and uttered his agreement. Isaac got to his feet, pulling Mitch with him.

Isaac kissed Mitch, meeting his eyes as he looked seductively through his lashes at him. "So you want to work up an appetite?"

Mitch grinned and let Isaac lead him inside. That sounded like a great plan to him.

Chapter 11

Isaac pressed Mitch back against the door as soon as it shut behind them. He knew it wouldn't last long, Mitch was a pushy fucker, but to start off he wanted to battle for control just because it was fun. Mitch laughed into the kiss and grasped Isaac's ass, pulling him close. They were both hard and needy. God knew how they'd made it to the room without giving in to kisses outside. They had an hour, and the sense of urgency was acute.

The kisses grew deeper, more burning, and all Isaac wanted to do was wrap his legs around Mitch and be carried to the bed. Mitch had done that at Christmas, actually physically hefted him onto the bed, and Isaac wanted that again. When Mitch gripped him hard and shuffled him back toward the bed, it wasn't exactly lifting, but Isaac scrambled away and onto the bed, yanking off his clothes and watching as Mitch did the same.

"Beautiful," Mitch murmured before kneeling between Isaac's spread legs and kissing him hard. "I want it all," he said into the kiss. "I want to take my time."

Isaac heard the unspoken words, the apology that this would be fast. Lack of time didn't matter; Isaac wasn't entirely sure he could hold out for long against the force of nature that was Mitch Stone.

"Next time," he said. "Just for now, let's do this…" He arched up into his own fist, and Mitch sat back and pushed Isaac's fingers aside and replaced them with his own.

"I haven't been with anyone else since," Mitch admitted as he pressed his face into Isaac's neck.

"Admit it, you just haven't had enough time," Isaac laughed. "It's barely been six weeks."

Mitch looked directly into Isaac's eyes. "You don't get it. I didn't want to. I wanted you, and I didn't even know your name."

Isaac smiled to soften his words. "That must have been some heavy shit wanting to track down a hooker—"

"An escort."

"Whatever, but tracking me down. Then what were you going to do?"

"Apart from the *Pretty Woman* thing? I hadn't thought that far ahead," Mitch admitted. He didn't sound pissed, or embarrassed, he was smiling as well. "I still kind of had this thing in my head for Dylan, you see."

"I see," Isaac said.

"But it's done, and I have you."

Isaac deliberately ran his tongue over his lower lip. "Naked, hard, and ready," he pointed out.

Mitch groaned and leaned down for another kiss. In a move that surprised Isaac, he nibbled down from throat to navel. Isaac had imagined they would rut and push and come in each other's hands, but this was different. Suddenly the barbecue was way down the list of things to do today.

"Mitch?" he asked in a daze. Before Isaac could even get his head around what was happening, Mitch sucked him down, no finesse, just a desperation that spoke volumes. Isaac whimpered and dug his fingers into Mitch's hair. He remembered that Mitch had loved this, pushing him to highs, forcing him to come even when he wasn't ready. Mitch was an expert at sucking cock, all lips and tongue and fingers.

"Isaac." Mitch pulled back, his lips swollen, his eyes wide. "Are you sure about this?"

Isaac closed his eyes and gripped Mitch's hair hard. Without saying a word, he guided Mitch's mouth back to his cock. Mitch didn't argue. He licked and sucked and used his free hand to caress Isaac's balls. He moved his mouth down to Isaac's sac briefly, then back up to concentrate on Isaac's neglected cock. Isaac stared down at Mitch for as long as he could, enjoying the view, until his orgasm took hold.

"I'm coming," he said urgently.

Mitch pulled off and Isaac arched up into Mitch's fist, the ropes of cum decorating his belly and Mitch's hand. He fell back on the bed, then tugged Mitch over him. Isaac immediately gripped Mitch's cock, and recalling Christmas, roughly brought Mitch to his own orgasm. In seconds the heat of Mitch's orgasm covered Isaac's hands.

They lay still, breathing heavily, but Isaac suddenly couldn't look Mitch in the face. He was stunned at what had just happened. This coming together was personal and real and not just about sex. This wasn't what he expected—hell, he'd thought he'd never see Mitch again. Then… this…

They grabbed a shower, the clock counting down until dinner.

"We could just stay in bed." Mitch smiled ruefully when his stomach rumbled.

"Food first," Isaac suggested. He watched Mitch as the man showered, admiring the gym muscles, the skin taut over hipbones, the cock half-hard and more than a handful as Isaac *helped* Mitch shower.

"You're going to kill me," Mitch said on a half groan.

"After Christmas? And everything we did? I don't believe your stamina is shot already."

Mitch chuckled and tugged at Isaac, pulling him under the water. "You realize they know exactly what we are doing up here? I saw Dylan watching us leave."

"And Bruno. He just gave me a thumbs-up."

"So we could legitimately stay in the room."

Isaac yawned and cuddled into Mitch. "I could sleep," he said. He knew it probably wasn't what Mitch wanted to hear, but he hadn't modeled in a while, so he ached and exhaustion threatened to take him.

"Food, then," Mitch decided. "Sleep after."

They made it to the grill just as Dylan was dishing up great slabs of meat and delicate fish while Adam fussed around the food. The spread of salads and breads was impressive, and Isaac helped himself to a plateful. No one speculated on what had happened between Mitch and Isaac, although Bruno winked and Dylan smirked. Bastards.

Isaac ended up sitting opposite Lucas and Bruno, with Mitch sliding in next to him. Dylan joined them with an impossibly full plate, and talk ranged from photography to the island.

"Tomorrow is the first half of the beach shoot." Bruno excused himself to leave. "I just want to get some prep out of the way. Thank you for the wonderful food." That left just the four men, and Mitch didn't say anything. When Isaac caught Dylan and Lucas exchanging a glance, he knew it was up to him to start the conversation.

"Can you tell us anything about the history of the island?" he asked.

"Tell them about the box," Lucas encouraged.

"What box?" Isaac was interested.

"We found this old box under the support for the shack near the waterfall. It was old and full of photos of a couple who used to be here on the island back in the forties."

"Wow, did they own the island?" Isaac couldn't think of anything more interesting than a mystery concerning old photos.

Dylan settled back in his chair. "I don't think so, but the couple were both men. Maybe they just spent time on holiday here."

"Kind of fitting really," Lucas said with a snort. "This island seems to attract gay relationships."

Dylan shook his head as he smiled. "Yeah, I know. Anyway, one of the men, his name was Peter, was rich and worked for his dad's charitable foundation. He married, then divorced. The other one was named Alfie. We don't know what happened to him, but we hope to find out more. Peter's great-grandnephew or something like that is visiting soon, and he says he has some diaries and old journals. We're still trying to track down Alfie's family, if there is any to find."

They talked for the longest time about Peter and Alfie, and only when Isaac felt himself drifting to sleep wrapped up in Mitch's arms did the small group disband for bed. The sky was black with diamond stars in stunning patterns and the trail of low lights to the hotel followed the path. When they got to the rooms, Isaac didn't even think about whether they were splitting to sleep alone. He was tired and he wanted to sleep in Mitch's arms tonight. Mitch appeared to get with the program and hustled Isaac into his own room, murmuring something about clean sheets.

When in bed Isaac snuggled into Mitch's space and inhaled his lover's scent. Lying there so close to

Mitch was perfect. Held tight, secure and happy, it didn't take him long to slip into an easy sleep.

Chapter 12

The large bonfire flickered in front of them. Smoke filled the air as the wood popped and crackled, shooting sparks onto the beach. A couple of the crew stood poised and ready with fire extinguishers. Mitch could only imagine the lawsuits if anything went wrong and one of the models found themselves doing an impromptu human torch impersonation.

Isaac was sitting beside him on the sand wrapped in a blanket as he watched Bruno and the models work. It was the final session, and Bruno certainly knew how to put on a show. Mitch just hoped it wouldn't go out with a bang too.

The sun was low on the horizon, setting fire to the sky and the ocean as it dropped from prominence. They seemed to have been blessed with the perfect evening. A palpable sense of excitement was in the air. Everybody had a smile on their face, even the usually pouty-faced Crystal as she was spun in circles by Yan. The models had been paired off, each couple prompted and given the freedom to dance around the fire, a conveyor belt of action as Bruno focused on each in turn. The women were an ethereal show of lightweight material and flowers, while the men looked wild and moody with dark makeup around their eyes and defining their cheekbones and jaws.

A pretty blonde whooped as she was swept off the ground by the male model with catlike eyes. Mitch wasn't sure he'd seen a position held so well since the last scene of *Dirty Dancing*. He admired the man's strong arms as he held the blonde high in the air. With pointed toes, the blonde moved gracefully, the material of her dress sweeping up around her. Her hair was fastened back from her face, and flowers were tucked into the braided line of her bangs. Eventually, she curled her legs around her partner and slid down almost snakelike his body until her feet were on the sand again.

"What do you think?" Isaac broke the silence they had fallen into, both of them fascinated by the display in front of them.

"I think..." Mitch paused and turned to Isaac. "I think it's beautiful."

Isaac looked at him. Mitch hadn't been talking about the staged shoot.

In the glow of the fire, Isaac looked amazing. The orange light was flattering and smoothed his already flawless skin. The temperature had dropped as they had moved into the evening, and sitting doing nothing had left Isaac seeking the warmth of a cozy blanket.

"Are you warm enough?" Mitch asked.

"I'm fine, thanks." Isaac tugged the blanket up over his bare shoulders. With a smile, he watched the models continue to strike their own poses. "I can't believe it's nearly over."

Had it really been a whole week, a couple of days longer for him and Bruno? Mitch wasn't sure he was ready to return to the real world, not just yet. His head and heart had been fighting a battle the last couple of days. He'd mostly ignored the call of his laptop and the emails he needed to answer. As much as he loved his job and the thrill of landing and sealing multimillion-dollar contracts, there was something equally exciting about stealing Isaac away from the models and crew and it being just the two of them. This thing between them was something new and different, and he wanted it as much as he'd ever wanted that closing signature. Human interaction, touch, love. He glanced at Isaac, then looked away. Mitch wasn't ready to go home.

"This time tomorrow we'll be home."

Mitch didn't appreciate the reminder. Following the shoot, there would be the obligatory *after party*, then a lazy morning, and by late afternoon they'd be heading home. What did it mean for the two of them once they left Sapphire Cay? "Isaac—"

"Isaac," Bruno shouted at the same time. "A few final shots, yeah?"

When Isaac didn't jump into action, Mitch knocked his shoulder with his own. "Go on. You should get some pictures."

Isaac didn't look so sure. It seemed that sitting majestically around a pool was one thing, joining in the quirky tribal routine was a whole other. "Really?"

"It's your last chance," Mitch told him. He flashed Isaac a smile.

"Do you want to join me?"

Mitch looked at Isaac, who was straight-faced. Was he being serious? "I think I'll pass. You're trying to sell clothes to people, not put them off."

"Oh, shut up." Isaac shrugged off the blanket. "Can Mitch join us for a couple?"

Bruno grinned, his red hair shockingly bright in the combined light of the evening and the fire. "Of course."

Mitch shook his head when Isaac held out his hands. He wouldn't say he was ugly or completely out of shape, but he sure as hell was no model. "I'm fine."

"Come on." Isaac crouched down in front of him. "Nobody but me and Bruno will see them." He glanced over his shoulder. "And I don't think anybody else really cares."

"Are you sure you wouldn't rather have photos with"—Mitch nodded to where the models were standing together waiting for their next instructions—"Adonis one, two, or three?"

Pursing his lips, Isaac shook his head. "Not right now."

Mitch sucked on his teeth. "Okay, but at the end, yeah? Get everything else you need first."

Disappointment dimmed the shine Isaac's eyes, but he agreed. "You promise?"

Mitch grinned. "Business first, right?" He was relieved when Isaac laughed.

"Fine. But you promised." He rocked back and pushed himself to his feet, then jogged the short distance to join Bruno and get organized.

"Wimp," Dylan said from behind him. He came and sat beside Mitch on the sand.

"No," Mitch said. "I just didn't want to steal attention from Mr. Middle Earth over there." He nodded to the blond male model, who was possibly prettier than Legolas.

Dylan gave a low laugh. "My mistake." He pulled his knees up and rested his arms on them. "It's been a good week. Everything seemed to come off smoothly."

"It has — well, nearly. You *do* remember Yan, right?"

Dylan laughed again. "Yeah, I remember Yan."

"It's been great," Mitch assured him. "Thank you for doing this."

"Thank you for thinking of us. Made a nice change from wedding after wedding."

Mitch wondered if diva models and their hissy fits were any different to the worst of the bridezillas. "It'll be yours next." He was slowly getting used to the idea that his old love was getting married.

"Don't remind me. I can't use you as an excuse anymore. There's only so long Lucas is going to let me get away with leaving it all up to him." He paused and looked at Mitch. "Which reminds me, we were wondering, hoping that maybe you'd come."

An invite? "Here? The wedding?" Mitch wasn't sure what to say. Did either of them really want him here? How would he feel seeing Dylan and Lucas married?

With a firm nod, Dylan insisted, "It'd mean a lot. As Lucas keeps telling me, my side's looking a little empty."

"You're just trying to fill seats," Mitch joked.

"Oh, no, I want you to give me away."

Mitch blinked. "What?"

Dylan's innocent expression was quick to fall as he punched Mitch on the arm. "I'm kidding."

"Dick," Mitch said. He rubbed at his chest. For a split second, he had believed Dylan. He frowned thoughtfully. "How does that work anyway?"

"What?"

"Being given away."

"Depends who wears the dress on the day."

Mitch screwed up his nose. Dylan in a dress was not an image he needed—lace bulging over broad shoulders. "I'm being serious." He'd never really thought much about the organization of weddings for same-sex couples.

"Well, we're walking in together. Both in suits," Dylan added.

"On the beach?"

Dylan pressed his mouth in a line and smirked. "Guess you'll have to turn up and find out." He looked over at the models beside the bonfire. "You've a plus one if you need it." He didn't wait to get a reaction from Mitch and quickly got to his feet and brushed the sand off his ass. "Right, I need to go and help finish setting up for this party of yours. Just think about it, yeah? I'll see you later."

With a sigh, Mitch looked back to where Isaac was surrounded by the models. If Mitch did attend the wedding, was it too soon to consider his plus one filled? There was definitely something between them. He had all these feelings, and Isaac had never shied away from reciprocating with his own. He smiled to himself as the models lined up. Isaac looked lost for a moment before being lifted and held horizontally on his side. When it was clear he wasn't going to be dropped, Isaac relaxed and smiled for the camera.

Whatever they had, Mitch wasn't going to deny his feelings existed. When Dylan had left him, it was because Mitch hadn't known what to do with how he felt. He'd stupidly chosen work every single damn time. But then he'd met Isaac. The man could fill the space in Mitch and still have more to give. Mitch worried at his lip. If he got this wrong and messed everything up, he wasn't sure there'd be anything left of his heart, not this time.

139

Was he strong enough to fight for Isaac? Or should their relationship end here on mutual terms and before either got in too deep?

Isaac laughed as he jumped down from the models' arms and bounded toward Mitch.

Love for the man tightened in Mitch's chest. Was he already too late?

"You ready?" Isaac asked.

Mitch nodded and stood up. He brushed down his cutoffs and let Isaac lead him to the fire.

"Okay," Bruno said and beamed at him. "Just want you to act naturally. Have some fun."

Act naturally? Mitch glanced around the group. When had all the male models lost their shirts? Isaac touched his face and he flinched, pulling away from Isaac's makeup-covered fingers. "What's that?"

"Just a little war paint." Isaac held Mitch's face with his other hand and drew lines across his cheeks and a single line down the middle of his chin. Happy, Isaac then wiped the rest of the makeup on his own face, a line down from his hairline to the bridge of his nose and lines on his cheeks to match the ones he'd drawn on Mitch's face.

Mitch was anxious. He wasn't supposed to be part of the shoot.

Had he said that out loud? Isaac was assuring him it was just some fun.

Apprehension melted away and Mitch relaxed, or he did until Bruno called for them to start. "What do I do?"

Isaac took him by the hands and pulled for him to follow. "Anything you want." He released one of Mitch's hands before raising the other to spin under Mitch's arm.

"Anything?"

Isaac nodded as he swung Mitch's arm to an imaginary tune.

With a rough tug, Mitch pulled Isaac by the hand. Their chests bumped together and all Mitch wanted was to kiss Isaac. Right now, there was nothing more natural to him than that, and Mitch wrapped his arms around Isaac's waist. Soundly, he kissed Isaac, leaning back to lift him from the sand. He held Isaac for a moment, enjoying the passion raging through him as they kissed beside the heat of the fire. Slowly, Mitch lowered Isaac to the ground and pulled away. Isaac smirked at him before spinning away from him.

Mitch watched Isaac, fascinated by his body in the red-orange glow. No matter what happened next between them, he was going to enjoy their last night together here on the island. With that thought secure in his mind, he gave chase across the sand and tackled Isaac.

They wrestled and laughed, and only when Isaac declared he had sand where there should be no sand did the two men walk back to Mitch's room hand in hand. Mitch was buzzing, happy, and everything felt absolutely perfect. They showered, keeping contact to just kissing. Whatever they did, it seemed Isaac wanted it to be as special as he did.

Naked and damp, they stumble-kissed their way to the mattress and tumbled onto it, laughing. For a few seconds, they lay as still as stone. Then Mitch felt Isaac's hand in his, and in a smooth move, Isaac crawled up and straddled Mitch. There were condoms and lube by the bed, and Mitch spent the longest time opening Isaac, stretching him and watching as Isaac rose and fell onto Mitch's fingers. He was a vision of sex and need, and Mitch wanted it all.

When he was deep inside Isaac, staring into Isaac's eyes in a connection that went past sex, Mitch realized he had already come to a conclusion.

He was not letting Isaac go.

* * * * *

"How many cocktails did you have?"

Mitch winced from beneath his shades as Isaac spoke. "Too many," Mitch declared. His head was pounding. He eyed the end of the pier, just visible from where they were sitting outside the hotel. The last of their things were piled waiting to be loaded onto the boat. He felt sick already, even without a boat ride in thirty minutes' time. Never had he regretted anything as much as he did the amount of alcohol he'd put away last night. He had no idea how he'd managed to have sex with Isaac, but he had, and fuck, it had blown his mind. Maybe it was some last-night fire in his belly, but they'd had an amazing time together, and from the looks a few others were giving them this morning, most of the island knew about it too.

"Do you want to go for a walk?" Isaac asked. "Just a little way along the beach while everything is checked onto the boat?"

As lovely as a stroll along the sand sounded, Mitch was enjoying the whole stationary, minimal-movement thing he'd got going on. "How about just down to the beach? We can sit in the shade on the sand and watch everybody else work."

Isaac looked around. Some of the team were sitting around, taking the opportunity to top up their tans for a final time. "Okay."

They walked to the beach hand in hand. Neither of them said anything until they were sitting cross-legged on the cool sand sheltered beneath the line of palms.

"I wanted to talk to you," Isaac said. Mitch guessed they were due a conversation, both returning to their busy lives in Miami. "I wanted to tell you how much I've enjoyed this week. It was better than I could ever have imagined. I didn't come here planning on meeting anyone."

Mitch let Isaac talk and didn't interrupt.

"This trip was always supposed to be about work. That's my life. That's your life. But for whatever reason, we found ourselves here together, and I'm glad we did."

Cursing last night's overindulgence, Mitch mustered his energy into saying the right thing, no matter what the outcome would be for them. "I'm glad we did too, and nothing is going to change that, but..." He leaned forward, stealing a kiss. "I guess we need to think seriously about where we go from here." He hated saying it, but like Isaac had said, work was their lives at the moment.

Isaac cupped his jaw and looked into Mitch's eyes. "What do you want?"

Mitch considered being all reason and sense but decided against it. "Dylan's asked me to come back for the wedding." He hesitated. "I have a plus one." He held Isaac's gaze, hoping Isaac wasn't going to make him spell it out.

"A plus one," Isaac mused. He stared out across the beach. "You thinking about asking anyone in particular?"

What the hell, right? Uncrossing his legs, he leaned forward and got on his knees. He crawled around to kneel in front of Isaac, surprised at the difference in temperature of the sand out in the open. He took Isaac's hand and said, "Isaac Bailey, will you be my plus one?"

Isaac laughed. "Cute."

"Well?" Smiling, Mitch waited.

"Okay, this is going to sound horrible, but…" He squeezed Mitch's hand. "I'm going to have to say maybe." He winced as he spoke.

"Maybe?" *Well, it isn't a no, I guess.*

"I'm so sorry. It's the week after the launch, and I have no idea what I'm doing. In my head there's all this buildup to the day, but when I stop and think about it, I realize it doesn't just end there. I know my dad has lined up some interviews with magazines, but I have been so focused on here and this shoot and—"

Mitch shut him up by pulling him into the sunshine and into a kiss. As the tension eased in Isaac's body, Mitch hugged him and then leaned back. "I'll take maybe."

Isaac smiled and lowered his head as a shadow fell on them.

Scott rested his hands on his hips when Mitch looked over his shoulder. "Sorry to interrupt. Everything's on board, well, apart from you guys and the others," he said. "Say, ten minutes while I round up the stragglers?"

"Yeah, that's fine." Mitch sat back next to Isaac. Scott flashed them a smile and then headed up the steps to the hotel, taking two at a time until he disappeared behind the trees.

They sat quietly for a moment until Isaac brought them back to reality. "That's it. Time to go." He leaned over and kissed Mitch before getting to his feet. "I left a bag at reception, so I'll see you on the pier, okay?"

Mitch nodded and let Isaac go. With a sigh, he stared at the ocean. Though he would never have expected it, now that it was time to leave, he was going to miss Sapphire Cay.

Chapter 13

They were separated by four rows of seats, and Isaac ended up sandwiched between the window and a woman who swore he looked familiar. After reassuring her that, no, he hadn't been on *Dancing with the Stars*, and no, he wasn't an actor, and yes, he just had one of those faces, he managed to open up a book on his Kindle and pretended to read.

Last night had been wonderful—the dancing around the fire, the cocktails, the mind-blowing sex—and now everything was back to normal with a bump. Isaac was sure that Mitch had wanted a yes to his question about being the plus one, and hell, Isaac had wanted to give it to him. But something was stopping him. Past experience was the most likely suspect, the crushing fear of rejection and disappointment. He wanted that indefinable 'more' and he wanted it with Mitch, but he just wasn't sure he was ready to open his heart to the man in case it got broken.

Idiot. I'm a goddamn self-fulfilling prophecy.

And now he was stuck here, way too far away from Mitch and wishing they'd thought to ask to swap seats. Mitch's expression when they boarded the plane had been guarded, and he'd been quiet, like everything that had happened on the island and the boat was being locked away and he was already distancing himself.

He wouldn't do that to me.

Isaac closed his eyes and turned his head toward the window, hoping he looked to be asleep. That would stop any talking or questions, and he could just ignore the way the woman—Sheila from Oregon visiting her daughter—was moving in her seat and pushing up against him with her ample behind. He really tried hard to ignore it all, but when she pressed a hand to his arm and squeezed some flesh, he reached a point where even his Southern charm wasn't happy. With an exaggerated huff, he opened his eyes and turned in his seat.

"Will you—" He stopped.

"Hey," Mitch said with a shit-eating grin.

Isaac blinked to clear his eyes. Where had Sheila gone? He looked over Mitch's shoulder. She was maybe in the bathroom? Then Isaac saw Mitch's bag on his lap and frowned.

"Did you switch?"

"I promised her your autograph."

"Why does she want my autograph?"

"Because she is convinced you were in a film with Brad Pitt."

"I told her I wasn't."

"Whatever." Mitch shrugged. "It got her to switch with me and now we have the rest of the flight to talk. And anyway, I hate flying and being next to you will distract me."

Isaac was happy about that. He wasn't sure he could have feigned sleep for the full hour flight back to Miami.

"More talking?" Isaac said with a soft smile.

Mitch leaned in conspiratorially. "I think even Sheila might be shocked if we make love in the seats, and I've seen the toilet and there is no way we're using that."

Isaac couldn't help the snort of laughter that left his mouth at the image of him and Mitch in the teeny-tiny bathroom. There was barely room to wash hands let alone find a position good enough to get off.

Shit. And now he was hard under his Kindle. The odd thought crossed his mind that Kindles weren't as effective as magazines for covering erections.

"What you smiling for?" Mitch asked.

"Don't ask."

"So yeah, I was looking at some stuff and knew I couldn't leave you up here all alone."

"I wasn't alone." It was Isaac's turn to lean in. "I had Sheila."

"Look." Mitch rummaged in his bag and pulled out his iPad. He powered it up and settled it between them. "Bruno emailed me raw shots, given how short the turnaround on this is, with the show only being three weeks away. I downloaded them on the airport wi-fi. He said they're just rough, but I thought we could see them together now to get an idea of what you may choose for publicity."

Mitch looked hopeful and Isaac realized he was staring directly into Mitch's eyes and not at the iPad at all. Impulsively he leaned over and kissed Mitch, nothing heavy, just a press of lips, but enough to let Mitch know how much he wanted him at that moment.

Mitch reached up and cradled Isaac's face, and they simply stared at each other for the longest time. Isaac wanted to blurt out "I love you." But he didn't. He couldn't. He'd be fooling himself if he didn't admit a big part of him expected to never see Mitch again.

Yes, they were both in Miami, but hell, it was a big city, and their lives were so very different. Mitch had his suits and ties and his meetings; Isaac, his muse and his designing and his fashion friends. Mitch hadn't offered the L word, so Isaac couldn't either. Not just yet.

Finally they looked down at the iPad and the slideshow playing there. In seconds Isaac was back on the island, and he could imagine the heat and the scents as slide after slide slid in to showcase his designs. Every so often he would pause the parade of pictures. There were some stunning shots here, of each of the models in the settings, the pool, the beach, the waterfall, then the bonfire, the last of the shoots.

As the slideshow came to an end, he saw Bruno had added in some candid shots: Lucas and Dylan talking with heads close, Adam pretending to pole dance on the gazebo upright, Scott with his head thrown back in laughter next to his partner. One of all the models pulling faces and the next with them all falling about laughing. Then there were some of him and Scott helping Adam down from the upright when his pants got caught, then a single one of Mitch smiling into the distance—a thoughtful smile and his hands pushed into his pockets.

"I like the next one," Mitch said.

When it appeared on the screen, Mitch pressed pause, and Isaac had time to examine every single part of it.

The picture was a casual shot of him and Mitch sitting next to each other by the fire. They weren't hugging or kissing, but it was the most intimate of the shots. Emotion choked Isaac. Mitch was looking at him with that perfect smile of his on his face, and Isaac was clearly in the middle of saying something. He was leaning in and laughing as he spoke, and Bruno had caught the expressions in the light of the fire, the oranges and reds playing on their skin. If there was ever a photo that summed up how Isaac felt, it was this one.

"That's lovely," Isaac said. Even as he said it, he realized how lame he sounded. Mitch was probably expecting more. "Stunning actually."

"I agree. Bruno is very talented."

"Can I get copies?"

"He won't want the client to have the raw shots," Mitch said immediately. "But the informal ones, I don't see any harm in that."

What time they had left was spent talking and flicking back and forth through the various shots. Isaac was damn excited about diving in and finalizing plans for the launch, and he blinked when the cabin crew informed them they were close to landing. The iPad had to be stowed, seats upright, and bags away. Isaac lost his props to hide behind. Mitch didn't comment, simply gripped his hand and interlaced their fingers. They remained like that as they landed at Miami International and only released the hold when the plane began to empty.

They moved through to baggage claim and were joined by the models who had taken the same flight and had a group of seats at the back of the plane. They were bright and chatting and excited to be home, and Isaac had never wished for peace more than at that moment so he and Mitch could get back to that sweet world they had found themselves in after looking at the photos.

"So, I'll see you soon," Mitch said when they were exchanging goodbyes.

"At the show," Isaac confirmed. He waited for Mitch to add that surely they would meet before that, but he didn't.

"I'll send you the shots."

"Thank you."

They kissed to the catcalls of the models. Just as Isaac was going to be honest about how he was feeling and damn the consequences, Mitch separated and jogged to the next taxi. He was going in the opposite direction into the city and had said he needed to stop at the office first. He waved, then was gone.

As simple as that.

Isaac climbed into the limo that was waiting for the group, and everyone shuffled about until they all fit. Then Miami International was in the rearview mirror, and real life headed toward him with a rush.

* * * * *

Mitch didn't know how he'd managed it. He had spent time on the plane, held Isaac's hand, kissed him goodbye, all while managing to protect himself by not saying "I love you." They'd only really been together a week, and no one in their right mind let on to another person that they wanted forever after that short a time. That kind of thing only happened in the movies. Mitch kept his love for Isaac close to his chest and resolved to give them distance before the show so Isaac could get back to the real world and have the time to think about what he wanted. He hadn't lost the conviction he had that last night in Isaac's arms, but he could admit that his confidence was shakier than it had been.

Burying himself in work was fine during the day. He even exchanged emails with Isaac about photo selection and printing without signing off with "I love you, I miss you." Isaac was busy, swamped with work, and his emails were so carefully worded that Mitch wasn't convinced that their time on Sapphire Cay hadn't been just a holiday fling.

Week one was the hardest. Every time an email pinged in his inbox, his heart lightened, which was ridiculous. He turned off the sounds his PC made with each new email when he realized he was slowly losing it and becoming conditioned by the noise to crave Isaac.

The second week was easier. They made plans for coffee, but Mitch had to cancel to meet with the marketing team on a new account. They made plans for breakfast before Isaac flew up to New York to spend time with his dad, but that didn't happen when the flights were brought forward. Still, they emailed, but even the emails were becoming less chatty. He didn't know whether that was because Isaac was getting nervous this near the showcase or if it was that Mitch was keeping his emails professional and therefore giving out the wrong signals. He deliberately signed off his latest missive about finished articles for print with "Miss your smiling face around here."

Isaac replied his okay with "Miss your hugs."

That was a good thing. Right?

Week three and Doris was avoiding his grumpy head. He was excited about the work he and Bruno had done on the showcase, all the articles were appearing that Jerry had worked on with Isaac last year, and on the magazine websites there was fresh copy and the gorgeous photos from the shoot. The photo that they'd chosen for the designer was a focused headshot of Isaac in one of his pure white Ts with violet geometric shapes around the neckline. The huge poster for the lobby at the show had been delivered to Mitch's office by mistake, and for an entire day he had a six-foot head staring at him through plastic wrapping.

Mitch could see every striation of color in Isaac's eyes, every fleck of amber in the brown, and Isaac was smiling as he stared out at Mitch. Part of Mitch didn't want to share this close-up look at Isaac with anyone else.

"He's a good-looking kid," Doris said from next to him, causing him to jump violently and spill his now-cold coffee down himself.

"Fuck's sake," he cursed.

Doris simply looked at him with raised eyebrows. "You're jumpy."

"Just didn't expect someone to be creeping up behind me."

She tapped the large photo with a long scarlet nail. "I was not creeping. I was standing there for a good minute before I spoke, only you were so focused on this you didn't hear me." She grinned.

"Sorry, just tired."

"Infatuated, more like." She leaned in and examined Isaac's eyes. "He has the most gorgeous eyes," she observed. "So we have an office pool that he's your boyfriend."

Mitch stiffened at the question. Doris might be his direct manager, but that didn't mean she could ask him stuff like that.

"No," Mitch snapped.

Doris nudged his arm, causing more coffee to slosh out over his hand. "You forget, Mitch, that you copy me in on all the emails you send to him."

Mitch wanted to protest that he'd stayed professional, but he caught the glint of amusement in his boss's eyes.

"Yeah, well, it's complicated," he muttered.

"How complicated can it be?" she asked. She took the cold coffee from him and ushered him out of the room toward the bathrooms. "Go wash off, then meet us in the viewing room. I have something to show you."

Mitch washed his hands and made a futile attempt to get the coffee out of his shirt and pants. When he checked in the mirror, it just looked like he'd wet himself. The hand dryer had enough hot air to dry most of it, but seemed he'd be relying on his cool calm confidence today and not his normally immaculate dress sense.

When he got to the viewing room, a large space with comfy chairs and a huge screen at one end, he found the core people concerned with Bailey's Clothing waiting. There was even fresh coffee.

"We have the final slides for the presentation that will run before the show." Doris waved at the screen. "One last look before we send it over."

Mitch settled back in his seat. He usually loved this part, seeing all the work coming together into a cohesive whole—tag lines, marketing points, pictures. Today, not so much.

He watched as dispassionately as he could, which was doing a disservice to the role he was supposed to be filling here. The show was gorgeous, how could it be anything but? The Cay was beautiful, the people pretty, the clothes dramatic and stunning. And there, just on the edges of some of the photos, was Isaac. Sometimes he wasn't even in the picture, but Mitch could recall exactly where he'd been standing when the photo had been taken. The agency had kept their promise, made sure Isaac wasn't the model in the photo, but apart from the models as the guy in charge. He looked so damn good.

They cleared the video for immediate dispatch, and everyone left the room except him. He made the excuse he needed to make a call. Doris smiled at him knowingly, but Mitch ignored her.

Tucked away in the dimly lit room, he dialed the only person who could make him understand this shit.

Dylan answered on the second ring.

"Sapphire Cay, Dylan speaking."

"Dylan, hey," he said. Then he quickly added. "It's Mitch."

"Hey, Mitch. Everything okay? You still coming out next week?"

Shit. He hadn't meant to make it look like he was backing out of attending the wedding. "Of course, man, I was just phoning for your advice. You have a minute?"

"Shoot."

"So I have this thing. With Isaac."

"Okay." Dylan didn't ask what the thing was, which was a step in the right direction. Maybe Mitch wouldn't have to explain very much at all.

"So, it's serious."

"Congratulations, Mitch," Dylan said warmly.

"No, I mean I'm serious. I've gone and fallen in love and I don't know how he feels and, shit, I feel like a teenage girl coming and talking to you like this."

Dylan chuckled. "So what did he say when you told him?"

"Told him what?"

"That you loved him."

"I haven't. I mean, I said I was falling in love. But the past couple weeks we haven't really connected except for one hug comment and that was pretty lame and I don't know how he's feeling and fuck—"

"Okay," Dylan interrupted. "Mitch, you want my advice. Tell him. What is the worst that can happen?"

"He laughs in my face."

"I saw the two of you together here—there is no way he's going to be laughing. He plainly adores you."

"He does?"

"You know what I saw? I saw him staring at you when you weren't looking, and I saw the way he would smile at you, the way you made him laugh, and the odd touches here and there. And you know what else? I saw you do the same thing right back at him. Tell him you love him, tell him you want more."

"Okay."

"Is he coming as your plus one to the wedding?"

"I asked him." Mitch didn't add the part about the whole Isaac being busy thing.

"Good. Now, stop talking to me and go speak to him."

"Thanks."

They ended the call, and for a few minutes, Mitch considered what to do. He could go over there now, track Isaac down at the hotel where the show was being held.

Or he could delay another day for fear of Isaac laughing in his face.

Instead he pulled out his cell phone and thumbed to Isaac's number. They'd exchanged numbers, but there had been no texting.

Hi, just saw your final presentation, looking good. Can't wait for tomorrow. He wanted to add a line about missing him again. But did that make him needy? "Fuck it," he cursed. *We need to talk. I really need you in my life.* Before he could second-guess himself, he sent the text. Then he waited in the dark.

The answer was quick, and he opened it to see the full message. *That's one thing not fucked up. Stage is only half set up. Freaking out. See you tomorrow.*

Mitch tried not to be disappointed that Isaac didn't address the emotive part of his text. Then another text came in. *You don't know how empty my life suddenly feels without you XXX.*

Mitch sent back three X's in reply. Then with a grin on his face, he went back to his office. This time tomorrow he'd be at the hotel, and he'd tell Isaac face to face exactly how he felt.

Chapter 14

Isaac stood back and folded his arms over his chest. Finally the stage was ready—a platform raised about five feet of the ground and jutting out into the old ballroom. The signature red and black was everywhere, and the Bailey's Clothing logo was in all the prominent places.

"Looking good," his dad said. He copied Isaac's stance, and they stood side by side staring at the stage. A couple of the models were sitting cross-legged halfway down the walk talking intently. The carpenters had left ten minutes before so the noise level had finally died down.

"I'm pleased." Isaac was the master of understatement at that moment. He was more than pleased. He was ecstatic, excited, nervous, sick, and, most of all, he was scared witless. People were going to be filling this place later—critics, fashion journalists, most of the cast of two major shows in Miami—all for his designs. He cast a critical eye over the big design board that Mitch's people had sent over. There was one of his design processes, blown-up sketches that showed inspiration and color. He was proud of that. The other was a six-foot-tall picture of his face. That he wasn't so proud of.

"You should be." His dad hugged him in an awkward sideways hug. "I'm so proud of you, son," he said, the words filled with emotion.

"Thank you for giving me the chance," Isaac responded immediately. He had been so lucky that he hadn't had to fight to get to here, not as a model or a designer. Of course the good luck was tinged with the frustration of not being seen as anything but an airheaded model, or even an escort. But still, he had luck and he knew it.

He smiled to himself at the thought of the best luck of all. Meeting Mitch. Mitch would be here soon, and finally, after weeks of emails, they were going to be face to face again. Seemed to Isaac that modern communication methods had a lot to answer for. Technology meant no one needed to meet in person this late in the project. Damn emails.

Who am I kidding? I avoided him.

"Your young man coming over?" his dad asked.

Isaac glanced at the time on his cell and nodded. They'd spent all last night exchanging texts, sharing memories of Sapphire Cay. They'd even sexted, which was hotter than Isaac could ever have imagined. Only when he'd come down from the high of an orgasm from an idea and his hand alone had he realized the power of suggestion that mere words could have. They hadn't called each other. There was something there stopping them, like neither of them were ready to commit.

But finally, in ten minutes, they would be face to face. And all Isaac wanted to do was commit in every way possible.

"I'll be in my room. Can you send him up when he gets here? We need to talk."

"Is he good for you?" his dad asked. "I haven't met him yet."

The admonishment in his voice was there, a gentle nudge that Isaac couldn't ignore. He had to be honest.

"I haven't seen him since the island," Isaac admitted. The words were like ash in his mouth.

"Why?"

"I wasn't ready to take that final leap. So I've avoided him since coming back."

"You're avoiding him in case he doesn't love you back?"

"I never said I loved him," he defended.

Robert Bailey chuckled. "You smile when you say his name, and you're clearly head over heels over him. He's going to be here and you want to tell him how you feel, but you're worried he's going to throw it back in your face?"

"I don't have an impressive track record with men. Remember Ralph and his homemade sex tape? Or that time with Andy and his freaking Twitter account?"

"I remember them both. But I also remember I never saw you smile about them the way you're smiling now when you talk about this Mitchell." Robert hugged him again. "I'll tell him you're waiting for him."

Isaac returned the hug and left the main ballroom, casting one last critical eye around the place. Then he made his way back to his room and let himself in to wait.

It didn't take long. The knock on the door was sharp and roused him from his thoughts. He opened the door, and his heart beat just that little bit faster to see Mitch.

For the longest time, they stood there. Mitch looked good, his suit perfectly tailored, the jacket open, his snowy white shirt buttoned, the whole look finished with a navy tie. His hair was immaculate and his skin smooth of the stubble Isaac had grown used to at the end of the week at the Cay.

"Hey," Mitch said softly. He rested a hand on the doorjamb and smiled. "Can I come in?"

Isaac stumbled back about as ungracefully as he could despite his training as a model. "Yeah, sorry," he apologized. Then he didn't know what to do.

"Last night—"

"I wanted to say—"

They spoke at the same time. Mitch closed the door behind him and leaned back against the wood.

"Go on," Isaac prompted.

"I just wanted to say… that I've been thinking a lot about us since we came back. I've missed you so much. Not having you next to me these last few weeks has been really hard."

Something akin to hope flared in Isaac's chest. Mitch made it sound like it wasn't just a beach fling, that it really could be more.

Isaac searched for the right words, but all he could say was, "Me too."

"You've been thinking too, or you've missed me as well?"

"Both."

They remained in a weird standoff. All Isaac wanted to do was say the words in his heart, but maybe he should just show Mitch how much he'd missed him. He moved toward Mitch at the same time Mitch moved toward him. They met in the middle in a heated kiss, and Isaac couldn't stop the words if he'd tried.

"I love you," he said between kisses. Mitch cradled his face and deepened the kiss.

"I love you," Mitch replied when they broke apart. "I've had this connection since—"

The kiss stopped his words, and Isaac deliberately moved backward in what he hoped was the direction of the bed, or at least the sofa. When his knees hit the mattress, he toppled them onto the bed. Finally sprawled out next to each other, they elbow-walked until they lay side by side.

"You love me," Isaac said with a soft smile. He snuggled into Mitch's hold and laid his head against Mitch's chest, listening to his lover's heartbeat.

"Yeah, couldn't really avoid it, kinda fell for you at the hotel at Christmas."

Isaac laughed. "You fell for a hooker."

"No, an escort. There's a difference." Mitch spoke so seriously and enfolded Isaac in the tightest of hugs.

"Big difference," Isaac smirked. "You wanna take this suit off so it doesn't get wrinkled?"

"I wish I could, but I have to get downstairs for final checks. Shouldn't you be down there as well?"

Isaac lifted his head and sighed. "Yeah. Just, we love each other and all I want to do is kiss you all over." Deliberately he cupped Mitch's groin and pressed just a little, enough to have Mitch push upward against his hand. Isaac wriggled up and straddled Mitch, his hands either side of Mitch's face. Then he leaned in, tilted his head, and kissed the man he had fallen so hard for.

"We need to go," he said, trying to be responsible.

"I may need a cold shower," Mitch muttered, although he was smiling, and Isaac couldn't resist one more kiss.

"Come on, then, let's go."

He waited patiently while Mitch rearranged and smoothed himself, then re-knotted his tie. Finally the two men were ready to go, and they left the room and called the elevator.

"You remember our last time in one of these?" Isaac asked innocently.

Mitch groaned again. "Stop that."

Isaac only waited until the doors shut before pushing Mitch into a corner and kissing him again. "Can't get enough of you," he whispered. "Love you."

The elevator stopped at their floor, but Mitch ignored it, staring straight into Isaac's eyes. "Love you. You ready?"

Isaac nodded. "Let's do this thing."

* * * * *

Mitch watched his lover, his boyfriend, as he led the event with a firm hand and a flair for the arts. The room was packed, and more than one person approached Isaac and handed over cards. He saw Isaac shake hands, talk to everyone, guide the models, answer questions, and he saw the life in the man he loved.

He found himself thinking about Dylan and Lucas. This must be how they felt, this tug that made Mitch want to go over and haul Isaac in for a hug. He felt an all-consuming need for Isaac and an overwhelming warmth inside him that meant he couldn't take his eyes off of the man he loved.

"Robert Bailey." A man stepped between him and Isaac. Instinctively Mitch shook the outstretched hand. He knew who Robert Bailey was — the owner of the clothing line but more importantly, Isaac's dad.

"Mr. Bailey," Mitch said formally.

"Call me Robert, seeing as you're going to be part of the family."

That got Mitch's attention. "I'm looking forward to that." He waited for the lecture about responsibility and not breaking his son's heart.

"Always be good to each other," Robert said instead.

Mitch could promise that. "We will."

Robert moved away, and Mitch's line of sight to the stage resumed. But there was no sign of Isaac. Mitch frowned as he tried to track his lover down, but then Isaac slipped a hand in his. He tugged Mitch away to the side of the room, and they ended up facing the six-foot headshot.

Isaac tilted his head and stared at the image. "Weird," he said.

"Gorgeous."

"I have lines."

"Laugh lines."

"Photo is too big."

"Not big enough." Mitch could play this game all day.

Isaac chuckled and laced his fingers with Mitch's. "Is that plus one for the wedding still on?"

"Hell yes."

"You gonna be sick on the boat again?"

"Will you love me still if I am?"

Isaac looked up at him, his brown eyes shining with emotion. "I'll hold your hair back."

Mitch pressed his hand to his chest theatrically. "That's the most romantic thing anyone has ever said to me."

Isaac shrugged. "Yeah, I know, I have my moments."

Mitch's analytical mind kicked in. "I'll book the extra plane ticket."

"I already did that."

"When?"

"The day after we got home."

Unspoken was the fact that Isaac hadn't stopped thinking about them for one second. Mitch wanted to say something that was as loaded as that simple statement. He really could only say one thing, though.

"I love you."

And from the way Isaac dimpled a smile at him, that was enough.

THE END

Capture the Sun

RJ Scott

RJ Scott lives just outside London. She has been writing since age six, when she was made to stay in at lunchtime for an infraction involving cookies and was told to write a story. Two sides of A4 about a trapped princess later, a lover of writing was born. She loves reading anything from thrillers to sci-fi to horror; however, her first real love will always be the world of romance. Her goal is to write stories with a heart of romance, a troubled road to reach happiness, and more than a hint of happily ever after.

Email: rj@rjscott.co.uk

Webpage: www.rjscott.co.uk

Facebook:
https://www.facebook.com/author.rjscott

Twitter: rjscott_author

Meredith Russell

Meredith Russell lives in the heart of England. An avid fan of many story genres, she enjoys nothing less than a happy ending. She believes in heroes and romance and strives to reflect this in her writing. Sharing her imagination and passion for stories and characters is a dream Meredith is excited to turn into reality.

Email: meredithrussell666@gmail.com

Webpage: http://www.meredithrussell.co.uk

Facebook:
http://www.facebook.com/meredithrussellauthor

Twitter: MeredithRAuthor

Made in the USA
Middletown, DE
06 February 2016